Willesden Herald

New Short Stories 3

Pretend Genius Press

London, New York, San Francisco, Seattle, Washington D.C.

www.pretendgenius.com

Published simultaneously in the United States and Great Britain in 2009
by Pretend Genius Press
London, New York, San Francisco, Seattle, Washington D.C.

This compilation copyright © The Willesden Herald 2009
Edited by Stephen Moran

ISBN 978-0-9778526-3-5

Acknowledgements

Many thanks to Rana Dasgupta and Pulp Net for their generous support of the international Willesden Herald short story competition. Thank you to the award-winning and brilliant writers collected here who celebrate the miracle of the short story and "ring the bells that still can ring."

Stephen Moran
Willesden, 2009

Contents

Jo Lloyd

Work

A while back, when I was going through a bit of a tough time, this guy I knew, Paul, bought himself a restaurant, and when it was still pretty new and he'd spent all his money on forks and skewers and real people who knew how to run a restaurant, he asked if I would help out, and I said yes because I didn't have a job and I didn't seem to be capable of getting a job and I didn't have a clue how to get myself out of the hole I'd fallen into.

I'll pay you, of course, he said. But I'm afraid it won't be very much.

And it was in fact a pittance that it was probably illegal to hire someone for, which was why it made sense to hire me. Later when I thought about it, and about how amazingly well the restaurant did, I thought he could probably have paid me more but I suppose that's how he got to be rich and I didn't.

I don't know what I had thought I would be doing,

perching on tables with a little notepad or making frilly garnishes out of lemons. But what I actually did was the things everyone else was too qualified to do, like mopping the floor and cleaning and then mopping the floor again and fetching and carrying and most of all washing up. And if you don't know I can tell you, washing up in a restaurant is hard. It's like being in the Titanic when it's sinking, only hot, and no Leonardo di Caprio to make things better. The dishes come crashing in around you and steam billows up in great clouds and sweat drips down you, actually drips, like rain on a window. I swear there must be a big room in hell which is just washing up and nothing else where they put all the people who didn't like to get their hands dirty.

I realized right on the first evening that this wasn't going to be any fun, but once or twice while I was still in the middle of realizing it Paul smiled at me in a harassed sort of way and said Good girl, as if I was a dog or 10 years old. I'd thought that the part of me that's meant to look into the future and want things was dead and gone, but there was obviously some murky corner where some little bit of it was still alive and had a teeny crush on Paul. So I wiped the sweatiest of the sweat off my eyebrows with the back of my sweaty hand and tried to look sophisticated and sexy and indispensable all at the same time.

Actually, I didn't get to see much of Paul, who spent most of his time Front of House, as he liked to say, selling expensive bottles of wine, which I did not know before but found out when I was working there is how restaurants make most of their money. Who I mostly saw was Gareth, who was the under chef, or Sous Chef as they would say, which is just under chef in French, which meant he spent all his time skinning things and gutting things and chopping things and every now and then sweating things, which is, funnily enough, what you call it when you fry onions or carrots or whatever so they're ready to turn into something more interesting, which I thought probably wouldn't happen to me even if I dripped over that sink for the rest of my life.

Gareth didn't complain. Gareth was a dopehead. He was lucky to have a job at all.

In fact, when you think about it, everyone there was lucky to have a job, and maybe Paul was actually some kind of a secret good samaritan and the ending up filthy rich was just a front and the restaurant was a place he made so that people like me and Gareth could be safe for a while.

Whenever we got the chance Gareth and I used to sit out by the dustbins smoking, and we got to be pretty good friends, as much as you can be friends with a dopehead. And what happened was we somehow formed ourselves into a kind of alliance against Paul, who was The Boss and therefore different from us. And Gareth said that that was a deep biological instinct, like monkeys or wolves or communists. It made me feel guilty, but after all Paul was still paying me the pittance and he wasn't even noticing me except sometimes to stick his head out the back and say Leave Gareth alone will you, he's got work to do. Which was insulting in at least two ways that I can count.

We were working what was called Split Shifts, which you might not have experienced if you've never had to do a lowly type job like that where you might as well be a donkey or a machine for all the life you get. It meant you did one shift in the day and one shift in the evening and in between was about two hours of free time to do absolutely anything in the whole world you wanted to do.

The early shift was usually pretty quiet. Not that there wasn't loads to do, getting everything Prepped, as they liked to call it, for Service, but it wasn't like it was in the evening, when you actually had to stop thinking just to get through it. Which is I suppose how donkeys and machines manage as well. In the day you could take a lot of breaks and Paul wasn't always there and the chef, Marcus, who was the boss of all of us except Paul, and even a little bit of him too, was often busy planning menus or whatever, which meant you got more of a chance to sit out back in the cool.

Gareth was older than me. He had that shrunk-in-the-wash look of people who've spent a long time being too busy taking illegal substances to eat. He always spoke very quietly and he used to do this funny little giggle, usually when there was nothing funny that anyone else could see. But it was good that he could find something to laugh about. Also, he talked, in that quiet voice, more than almost anyone I've ever met, including 12 year old girls. On day one, when I barely knew him at all, he told me practically his whole life story, which is a thing that I have noticed with people who take a lot of drugs, they have no discrimination, they don't distinguish between their intimate friends who'd hold their head and their hands and their hair for them and someone who just happens to be sitting next to them scrounging their rollups and watching the flies buzz around the bins.

One part of his life history that Gareth told me that day was about his childhood. His mother died when he was very young and he went all over the world with his father, who was something to do with the war against mosquitoes, which sounded pretty important to me. But Gareth said it was actually a little spat that distracted people from the True Struggle. And it meant Gareth got moved about from place to place like luggage and never had a home. And I thought all that moving might have added to his ordinary dopehead kind of indiscrimination, because another kind of people who can't make friends properly, I have noticed, is people who've travelled a lot.

Another part of his life history that he told me that day was about a girl he'd been in love with. She was his soulmate, he said. When he knew her she was very sad, for reasons I couldn't quite grasp, but god knows there's enough bad things out there happening to someone, try making a list, it's a wonder there's anyone left who isn't sad.

He used to send her poems and put flowers through her door and she treated him very kindly, like a little brother. She had all these suitors and ex-suitors that she was too sad to go out with, but she liked to have them around her. That sounded pretty weird to me but he saw nothing wrong with it, except that it made him unhappy. And he got more and more unhappy and eventually he took an overdose. He woke up in hospital and for a while he forgot how to speak. And this girl would come and sit with him and they wouldn't speak at all but she understood him, so he thought anyway, I have my doubts. But you can form an idea like that, that there is only one person and one time and one place where you could live, and then for the whole of the rest of your life you'll feel homeless.

He told me about all the jobs he'd done too. He'd worked as a postman for a while, but it involved a lot of rules, which had to be followed to the letter, ha ha, and he'd got sacked for emptying the postboxes in a different order, which it turns out is about the worst thing you can do if you're a postman. Then he'd been a delivery driver, until one day he was on the motorway, and a lorry pulled out, and a car cut in, and I imagine with all the dope his reactions weren't as quick as they might have been, and it was ok, nobody crashed or anything, but he realized he was basically spending his days in a race to the death. So he came off at the next exit and turned the van round and took it to the beach. Then he'd got a job in an electronics factory. Most of the other people were women because the job involved putting together fiddly little things, which they do better with their small hands. And that suited him very well because there was music playing and you could talk. But then the company found a way to do it cheaper using machines or small-handed Chinese children. They asked for voluntary redundancies, so suddenly everyone thought someone else should go, the older ones or the younger ones or the single ones or the married ones, depending who was thinking it. They turned against each other, which Gareth said was how Capital kept people in a state of semi-consciousness. Anyway, the end result was Gareth was out. After that he'd got his first job in a kitchen, and he liked that ok, there was no driving and he thought it would be pretty difficult to come up with a machine to replace him.

I didn't get all of this the very first time we talked, but a surprising amount of it, and then more got filled in later and some of the same things repeated, along with a bunch of trivial stuff about the time or the weather or something someone had said just a minute before which is, after all, the stuff that takes up most of every day of your life, whatever it is you're doing.

As it turned to winter it got pretty chilly but we still sat outside when we could. If you've never felt it, I can tell you it's a vile feeling to go out all sweaty hot, and then get cold so the sweat clings to you like slime, and then you go back inside and it's like you've been painted with some caustic chemical that's slowly peeling off. I don't remember them mentioning that sort of thing in Careers.

But on the whole, it was going ok for me. Another thing I didn't know before and only found out while I was there, is that when you're doing that kind of don-key work and you're so tired at the end of it that you haven't got the strength to keep up your usual barriers, you get close to your fellow donkeys pretty quick and you have a warm glowing feeling toward them, as if they were your actual friends. So there was that, and then I was sort of getting used to the split shifts, more or less, and by now I'd given up on Paul being anything other than The Boss, and the tiny pittance was making a tiny nibble into the big pile of debt I'd accumulated. Plus, most of all, I was starting to feel like maybe I could be a person who could have a job. And that was quite a leap forward for me.

When I say about this warm feeling, it wasn't like that with everyone of course. There were some people you just couldn't stand, and for Gareth and me it was the chef, Marcus. People come and go in kitchens pretty fast, but Marcus had been there from day one and didn't look like leaving any time soon. Of course, as I said before, he got to boss everyone around, so it was a good job if you're the sort of person who likes that. And he was.

Marcus was older than all of us, with grey hair, and he had that look some men have of seeming to have a moustache without actually having one, which I have always thought makes a person seem sly and untrustworthy. He was an alcoholic or maybe an ex-alcoholic. And he was very tall and what you might call gaunt. It's funny that we were dishing out all this cream and butter and treacle pudding but everyone who ever worked in that kitchen was skinny as a dog in a war zone and looked like they were starving right there in the middle of all that food, like there was some vitamin required for normal living that their body couldn't process.

Marcus was a bit of a tyrant, but it turns out it's practically obligatory that the chef should act like a sergeant major or the teacher that everyone hates. And of course I was so lowly he didn't speak to me that much.

But Gareth was Marcus's second in command, his Sous Chef, and Marcus ordered him about like his very own personal Sous Dog. And Gareth said Yes Chef no Chef three bags full Chef just as promptly as anyone, but when he was out back he would sometimes be simmering, you could see it, all worked up so he had to sit with his eyes closed humming until it was time to go in and get shouted at some more.

Gareth never argued or complained or sulked or even twitched an eyebrow, but there was this one thing he would do that you could see really got to Marcus. It was pretty much a rule there that everyone got in early. It was part of the whole thing where we were all supposed to be sucking up to Marcus like all we had ever wanted was to wear his fancy hat. But what Gareth would do was he'd turn up early but not go in. He'd stay out front, sitting on the wall opposite the restaurant, and just wait. We all knew he did it because we would have to walk right past him, and Marcus knew that we knew because Marcus himself would have to walk right past him. Then right on the dot, Gareth would come in, not even half a second late, so Marcus couldn't say anything at all. And you could see it ate him up. And then he'd shout at Gareth a bit louder during the next service, and then Gareth would have to keep his eyes closed and hum a bit longer, and so it went on.

So it got to be December, and some people had left and some new ones had come, and one of the new ones was Mair, who used to sit out by the bins with Gareth and me. Mair worked there part-time, when her ex could have the kids, and she was one of the sweetest people you could ever hope to meet. She was a recovering anorexic – she said she was recovering, although I never saw her eat – and she looked as if she'd snap in two if you touched her and also she had scars on her arms from where she used to cut herself with knives and scissors and probably the whole Batterie de Cuisine. She said she didn't do that any more, so there you are, people do get better sometimes.

Gareth liked Mair. Which meant, it turned out, that when she was around he stopped speaking, so you started to see where he'd gone wrong in his former relationships. He did, however, at some point pluck up the courage to say something to her and she said no way no, you're kidding aren't you, only more kindly than that I'm sure. She told me afterwards that what with the kids and the job and the ex and some guy who came over sometimes, she had quite enough to take care of already.

Gareth didn't say anything about it, but you saw him sometimes looking at her quite mournfully.

So Gareth and Mair and I were out back one day. It was getting towards Christmas, lots of office parties wearing paper hats and tinsel like they were in some kind of weird ceremony. They laughed a lot but they looked scared out of their minds, of what I don't know, of what they were laughing at, or the people they were laughing with, or how another year had gone by and here they were celebrating it. Anyway, they made a lot of extra work for us, getting blotto and throwing silly string and ordering everything in sight because they weren't paying for it, and we were all even more tired than usual and most of us weren't exactly looking forward to Christmas.

So when Marcus came out telling us to quick march into the kitchen and stand to attention no one felt much like moving and he had to come out again. And probably because she was the most timid of us, he started on Mair. Do you want this bloody job or not? he said. And you could see Mair was going to jump up and go in, and normally that's what we'd all have done. But maybe because it was Mair, or maybe because it was Christmas, or maybe because of the True Struggle, Gareth put his hand out to stop her and said, We're taking a break. We'll be in in a minute. He didn't even say Chef.

Marcus looked taken aback for a second because no one ever ever ever answered him back and then he said You'll be in when I bloody say.

We'll just be a minute, said Gareth.

You've had warnings, said Marcus. Which was news to me.

Gareth didn't say anything and Mair and I didn't know what to say.

Maybe none of you want this bloody job, that can be arranged, said Marcus, and he turned round and walked back in and after half a second Gareth got up and said This isn't on, and followed him in. And Mair and I looked at each other and she said Oh shit. And then we went in.

We could hear Marcus shouting in the cold room, with silences that must have been Gareth answering very quietly. I thought it might be a good idea to give the floor another mop and Mair started on the veg. Then Paul came in and wanted to know what was going on and everyone just looked at each other and said nothing and Paul went into the cold room and then very soon after that all three of them came out of the cold room and went out into the dining room in a single file, Paul first and Marcus last with Gareth in the middle and no one saying anything any more.

I never found out if Gareth was sacked or if he resigned. I asked Paul and he refused to discuss it. He's not coming back, he said, and that was all he would say. And I asked for Gareth's phone number but he wouldn't give it to me, so I had to go into the office when he wasn't there and look for it. There wasn't a phone number, only an address, so I wrote it down on a page I tore out of Paul's desk diary, which was blank and just for show or because someone imagined it was the kind of thing you would need to run a business, which wasn't true, it seemed to me, obviously what you needed was a cold hard heart.

A couple of days later, between shifts, I went to the address I had written down. I had to take two buses and I wondered how Gareth had managed that every day as well as everything else. He lived in a bit of town that was probably nice when Queen Victoria was on the throne and no one had bothered making any repairs or even cleaning it since. Everything was slumped, and half the windows were boarded over and most of the rest were covered with that thick grey dirt that takes years to build up.

Gareth lived on the top floor of a place that had about 10 doorbells although it didn't look big enough for that number of fully grown people. I rang his doorbell and when nothing happened I rang the rest of them but no one answered, so either they were all out at work which didn't seem likely or they thought I was the bailiffs or the social or someone else who might prise them out of the hole they'd managed to wedge themselves into hoping to wait it out until the tide came in.

But then this woman opened the door, not to let me in, but to come out herself. You could see immediately she was one of the ones who'd gone altogether. She had shopping bags full of stuff that was not shopping, and no teeth, real or false. She looked at me suspiciously, but probably she looked at everyone that way, it wasn't that she recognized me as one of her own.

I went past her through the open door and up the stairs to the top, where you had to stand one step down and reach up to knock on the door. I hammered away for a while and I shouted through the door that it was me. And that was the end of my ideas. But then I heard a shuffling inside, and Gareth opened the door. And he looked so pleased to see me, I felt bad for not being more pleased to see him.

He looked like he'd aged 10 years. He hadn't shaved, and his eyes were red, and he was wearing pyjamas with an old, worn coat over the top, like one of those shell-shocked convalescing soldiers out for a walk in the grounds.

We went into the kitchen, which was also I suppose the sitting room, it had a couch in it, which we didn't sit on, but no table. Do you want a drink? Gareth said, but he looked anxious when he said it which made me think he might not have anything to drink, or not enough to give away at least. I was standing next to the cooker and there was a pan there with some soup in it, a bit of thin soup which didn't look like it would nourish a dormouse.

I asked if he was alright. He looked at me like he was still listening to bombs exploding somewhere off in the distance. I told him what had been going on at work, how upset Mair had been, what Marcus and Paul and everyone had been doing. He said some things which seemed unconnected. I talked about the bus journey. And the weather. Asked what he was going to do.

It seemed that everything we had talked about together, that had been like a cosy blanket we were knitting between us, each of us with a pair of needles, clickety click, all of it had been left behind the bins, and we had to start all over again.

Then Gareth said You're a kind person. Which I knew I wasn't. And he came over to me and leaned, keeping his feet in place, just leaned, until he was resting his head on my shoulder. And I didn't know what to do but I felt panic coming up in my throat like moths so that I couldn't speak. Him leaning on me in this way, as if I could possibly bear his weight, as if I could stay upright under it, as if I wouldn't fall over into the dormousy soup at any minute, was intolerable. I had to stop it.

You'll be fine, I said, which was patently not true. He kept leaning and I said I have to go now, I have to get to work. And the word landed at the end of the sentence with a big thud, as if I was just rubbing it in that I had somewhere to go and he didn't.

He did a kind of reverse lean then, lifting his head off my shoulder and returning to perpendicular, and he stood in front of me, in his pyjamas and his coat, swaying a little.

You'll come again, yeah? he said.

Of course, I said. I mean, if I can. Of course.

And of course, I didn't. And in fact I never saw him or heard of him after that. And even now it makes my stomach hurt to think about what might have happened to him and to know I didn't help or even try to help but just went back to Paul and Marcus and mopping the floor, as if there were sides and I'd picked one.

I kept working in the kitchen for quite a long time after that, until hardly anyone remembered I hadn't always been there, and half the time I hardly remembered myself. Mair left, and other people left, and even Marcus left in the end. But whoever was there, however things changed, somehow it very quickly felt to me like it had always been that way, and always would be.

Gareth wouldn't have been surprised by that. He used to say that work is like dope. The Dope of the Masses he used to call it. Sometimes it makes you high, and sometimes it makes you sick. But mostly it just softens the edges, so you won't wonder what your days are for, or notice that they're passing.

Carys Davies

The Travellers

The last time it happened, I packed my bags and left. I got on a train at Birmingham New Street and then on another and another and another and I didn't get off until I reached Siberia.

I liked Siberia.

I liked the snow, the quiet.

I opened an inn at the edge of a small town, and catered for the passing trade - a good kitchen with hot stew and boiled potatoes, a downstairs room with a fire and high-backed benches where people could warm themselves and eat their dinner. Upstairs there was a dormitory with six plain but sturdy bunks, and for those in search of a little privacy who were prepared to pay me the extra, two more rooms, each with its own carved and painted single bed. I found a local man, Pyotr, to help me with the heavy work, chopping wood for the stove and the fire and lugging it in from the shed, shovelling snow and seeing to people's horses, repairing their sledges etc.

I prospered; I didn't miss Birmingham, I didn't miss any one from the office, and whenever I found myself thinking about Geoffrey, well, I just busied myself with something that needed doing, like peeling vegetables or polishing the samovar, or shaking out the big floppy mattresses on the beds upstairs.

My new life was calm.

It was uneventful, and even if I wasn't exactly happy I was at least doing okay. Pyotr was proving himself to be hard-working and reliable and I had settled into a routine; I was enjoying the cooking, my Russian was coming along nicely. I'd started learning the balalaika.

And then, one cold winter's night, very late, when I had washed down the tables and wiped the greasy remains of the meat from the wooden board in the kitchen, when everything was quiet - the six guests who'd come earlier were asleep in their bunks in the dormitory upstairs, the young lawyer who was on his way to Vladivostok was tucked up in one of the single beds, an elderly insurance salesman from Irkutsk in the other – I heard the sound of a sledge, drawing softly to a halt outside the front door.

Pyotr swore; he had just finished tying on his hat, ready to go home. 'It's all right, Pyotr,' I said. 'You go. I can do the fire.'

But Pyotr didn't move; he was staring at the door. I felt a blast of cold air in my back, snow spiralled into the warmth on the freezing wind, a shower of icy flakes landed on my neck and when I turned there he was, steam rising like smoke from his tall fur hat and his long frozen coat: a huge black-haired man, dark and wild like a Cossack, with a beard and a broken nose and narrow glaring eyes and a thin furious mouth - the meanest, most murderously bad-tempered looking person I had ever seen in my life. In one gloved hand he carried a large bone-handled knife with a curved blade that dangled almost to the floor; in the other - a piece of brown paper crumpled into a twisted cone, like a small flowerless bouquet, or the losing end of a Christmas cracker. He asked for vodka.

Pyotr and I began to scurry about, Pyotr going out to the shed for wood to build up the dying fire and back out again to see to the man's horse. I heated up what I had left of the stew and poured vodka into a brown jug and worried about how I was going to tell the terrifying Cossack that I was full for the night, that I had no beds left. Perhaps I could go up and ask the young lawyer if he wouldn't mind squeezing into the dormitory if I put a mattress on the floor and gave him back his money in the morning?

Perhaps –

But I got no further with sorting out the bed problem, because just then Pyotr came back into the kitchen and I knew at once that he had some news to tell me. He was a close, silent sort of man, Pyotr, some one who, though he swore quite a lot, actively seemed to dislike having to speak. On this occasion however I could see that there was something urgent and unavoidable he felt obliged to communicate.

He stood for a while, stamping his boots on the mat to get rid of the snow and untying the laces of his hat from around his chin so that the furry ear flaps hung loose on either side of his broad head.

'What is it, Pyotr?' I said. 'What's the matter?'

He nodded towards the other room, where the

Cossack was, and over to the little window near the front door.

'A woman'.

'A woman?'

Pyotr nodded. 'Outside. On his sledge.'

I looked. I craned my neck to see over the high backs of the benches in the other room. It was true. There was a shape on the sledge, I could see it through the misted window, hunched into a ball against the whipping of the snow, motionless as a pile of rags.

Over by the fire the Cossack had finished his stew and, by the look of it, the jug of vodka too. He was staring into the flames, brooding and cross. He had taken off his long coat and I could see the curved knife, hanging now from a leather loop attached to the coat's belt.

'Is she dead?' I whispered.

Pyotr shrugged.

I tried to get a better view through the window by rising up on my tip-toes. It was a distance of about twenty feet from the threshold of the kitchen, where I was standing with Pyotr, over to the far wall of the front of the inn where the window was – a small, frost-feathered window with eight thick panes of glass just to the left of the solid front door. To our right, another twenty feet or so away, sat the Cossack, on one of the benches by the fire. Very softly, I took a step out of the kitchen into the room. There. I could see her more easily now. Although it was late, the light was good, the moon shone and the snow was bright, and as I looked, as I craned my neck again to see over the lintel of the window, I thought I saw the heap of rags move.

'Pyotr,' I whispered and nodded towards the window.

This time there was no mistake. The bundle shifted and we saw her face, long and pale like an almond and wrapped tightly round in a dark fringed shawl. Just for a moment, she looked towards the inn; then turned away again and sat like before, motionless and staring straight ahead at some distant point in the snow.

Pyotr was shaking his head and looking uncomfortable. He hated getting involved in the lives of others and had started tying on his hat again.

'Don't go, Pyotr,' I said. 'Please'.

He looked back over at the Cossack, at the knife hanging from his coat. Pyotr shook his head again and took off his hat. I wondered if there was something he wasn't telling me - if he understood these people better than I did and just didn't want to say. You could never quite tell with Pyotr. It was almost impossible to tell what he was thinking at any given moment; what he did or didn't know.

'Do you think he's kidnapped her?' I whispered.

Pyotr shrugged like before. 'Possible.'

I pictured the huge angry Cossack grabbing the woman by the hair while she was walking down the street and forcing her onto his sledge then bringing her here to my little way-side inn against her wishes. I wondered if he was some sort of mercenary - if he had stolen her to order perhaps, and planned to take her in the morning to a secret destination where he would be paid for her delivery. I wondered -

Pyotr nudged me with his elbow. I jumped.

The huge man was on his feet again. Behind him on the low table in front of the fire lay the crumpled piece of brown paper he'd been carrying when he'd first come storming in. He had smoothed it out. I wondered what it was. A letter perhaps? Some sort of contract? A set of instructions? Something, at least, that formed a connection of some sort between him and the woman?

He was standing now with his back to the fire. I could see his face. He had pushed his wild black hair back from his forehead and as we watched him through the open kitchen door, he rubbed his cheeks and forehead vigorously with his big hands, as if he were washing his face - the way people do when they are tired and want to revive themselves before beginning some new and necessary task. He let out a big sigh. Then he put on his coat, walked over to the door, and went back out into the snow.

It was falling more thickly now. The woman, in her shawl, had begun to resemble a big white stone. A black dog had come trotting out from the town and was sniffing around at the base of the sledge.

I opened the front door a crack behind the man. The wind had died away and when he spoke we heard him clearly.

'You will freeze', he was saying to her in a flat toneless voice. 'In the morning I will come and you will be nothing but a block of ice. A frozen statue.'

I could see now that she was very beautiful, but also that she was as angry as he was. Both of them had exactly the same expression – sullen, furious, unyielding. She hated him and he hated her back. You could feel it, plain as anything, the poison between them – a bitter, resentful mutual loathing that seemed ready at any moment to turn into something much, much nastier.

The Cossack took a step forward, the dry snow squeaked beneath his boot. 'You should come in now,' he said.

The woman raised her chin. 'No.'

'Then you will die.'

His words hung between them in the freezing night; it occurred to me that it was the cold and nothing else that had brought him out to her. It wasn't because he wanted to be the one to make peace between them; everything about him was grudging and reluctant; he was as morose and brimful of dislike as she was; it was only the danger she was in that had made him come out - the dark travelling shawl she had on might have been good enough for the day but it would not see her through the night. He stood there for another few minutes while she remained seated on the sledge, mulishly still as before. At one point he held out his hand to her in a cool, unwilling kind of way but when she didn't take it he let it fall, and in one final furious gesture, he took off his coat and threw it, knife and all, onto the sledge, so it covered her shoulders like a blanket, and then he came marching back into the inn, alone.

Inside, on the low table by the fire, the piece of brown paper lay as before. The man picked it up now, folded it, and put it away inside his shirt. He didn't ask if I had a room, he just wrapped his giant's arms around himself and leaned against the high back of the bench and sat there, glaring into the fire.

Sometimes I wonder if at some half-conscious level, I knew then what had happened between them.

If I did, I wasn't aware of it; when I discovered the truth, it came to me, I swear, as a revelation.

I didn't go to bed. From time to time during the night and early morning I looked out through the window at the woman on the sledge. It was one of the drawbacks of the inn that we had no covered place for the horses and the sledges, only an open shelter with a beaten tin roof which kept out some of the wind but not the cold and not much of the snow. She wasn't wearing the man's coat. It lay behind her like a big dead animal. Still she sat, straight as a pole, though as the hours passed, her body began to shake. Around two o'clock the snow stopped falling; it was too cold now for snow. A crust of ice formed on the leather traces of the sledge and around the woman's shawl and on the tops of her boots.

Twice in the night I went out with Pyotr, once with a fur wrap and once with some stew; she thanked us for both but when I said, would she come in out of the cold and sit by the fire? she shook her head.

'Not if he's in there.'

Towards morning we went out for the last time.

The stone pillars of the town gates were grey against the yellow sky, snow filled the thick clouds but none had come down now for several hours. Something had happened though, to the woman.

She lay now, in the bottom of the sledge. The black dog that had come in the night sat on her feet, as if trying to keep them warm. But she was frozen hard; her hair, when I lifted a piece that had slipped out from her shawl onto her face snapped between my fingers like a frozen reed. I prised open the crisp folds of her clothing – the fur wrap, her grey woollen shawl – and found her hands. I began to chafe them with snow.

Pyotr watched, frowning. 'Stop,' he said. 'Let Pyotr.'

He was strong, Pyotr. Short and stocky and wide. Even so, he couldn't move her. He put his arms around the lumpy parcel of her body but it seemed to cling with a kind of obdurate force to the sledge. She was frozen and stuck to it. He went inside and came back with a rope, looped it around her and pulled. There was a sharp snap as she broke free from the ice and then he lifted her in his arms and carried her, like a small frost-covered pine tree, into the warm.

The fire was low now, there were just a few embers left glowing in the grate. Mostly it was ash. I raked up what was there and threw on a new log. The Cossack was still sitting up but he was dozing now. Pyotr laid the frozen woman at his feet by the hearth.

Under the fur wrap and her woolly grey shawl she had on one of those pretty, brightly embroidered dresses, like the ones the Sadler's Wells dancers had worn when Geoffrey took me to see *The Rite of Spring* a few years before for my birthday. The most striking thing about her, though, was her face, still furious and indignant, gazing out from beneath a thin carapace of ice, like something trapped in a pond, or behind the clouded glass of an old mirror. The effect was curious and unsettling; it was clear to me now that she was dead.

On the bench beside me the Cossack no longer slept. He was sitting without moving, just staring at the body of the frozen woman at his feet.

Pyotr grunted. He bent to the floor to pick up his rope, which was lying in a sodden coil on the hearth. I didn't know what to say. For something to do I began to gather up the remains of the Cossack's dinner - his bowl and cup, his fork and spoon, the empty vodka jug - and perhaps it would all have ended there if I hadn't noticed then the piece of paper on the floor beneath the bench, the one the man had carried in his fist and later folded and put inside his shirt. It must have fallen out while he slept.

I picked it up, opened it. It was a map. A maze of hand-drawn tracks across the snowy wilderness, an arrow in the right hand corner, pointing north. I thought of the Cossack's smouldering fury when they arrived, of the woman's suicidal six-hour sulk in the snow and then I understood; everything that was familiar about the two of them seemed at that moment to reveal itself. Even before the Cossack glanced over and saw me holding the map, even before he'd shrugged his massive shoulders and thrown up his hands and gestured towards the window at their sledge parked outside, even before he'd opened his mouth to speak, I knew what he was going to say:

'Always when we drive, my wife and I, we argue.'

I thought of Geoffrey.

I thought of our last horrible scene in the car after his brother's wedding in Salford, after I'd told him to come off the M6 just north of Manchester at junction 26 and go into Wigan; after we'd got lost in Wigan and been stuck in traffic for an hour and three-quarters in the centre of town, then trailed slowly on for another hour through Hindley, Atherton and Tydesley, and ended up arriving at the church when the wedding ceremony was just finishing; I thought of how we'd sat through the reception without speaking a word to each other and then walked silently back to the car, of how Geoffrey had taken the road atlas out of the compartment in the door on my side and said to me in that quiet voice that pretends to be patient and understanding but is in fact a hair's breadth away from being speechless with incandescent fury, 'Why would you do that, Harriet? Why wouldn't you tell me to come off at junction 21a and then take the M62 all the way up to the M602 into Salford? Or junction 20 so I could have taken the M56 and picked up the western ring road until we hit the M602 there and gone in that way? *Jesus Christ, Harriet,* why would you take us in through the centre of Wigan on a Saturday morning?'

I remembered how I'd turned away from him and stared out of my window at the trees and the departing wedding guests and the other cars in the hotel car park and said, quietly, as he had, 'It seemed like the best way to me, Geoffrey.'

I thought of the five hours we'd spent on the Boulevard Périférique in Paris. I thought of the horrible, fat Michelin book with its hundreds of pages, each one with a small piece of Paris on it so that the road kept running off the edge of one page and on to another but never onto the next page, always onto a different page somewhere else in the book that you could only find by consulting the index at the back and by the time you'd found it, it was too late. I thought of Geoffrey's demented shouting as we went whipping past the Saint Cloud exit for the fourth time. *Shall I come off here, Harriet? Shall I? Shall I? Tell me what I need to do Harriet, you need to tell me, you need to tell me, you need to tell me NOW. Look! There's the exit. You need to tell me now now now now now oh too late.* I thought of the evening we drove down to London for a seven thirty performance of *Oklahoma!* at the National Theatre; of how at around eight o'clock, somewhere between Hendon and Cricklewood, Geoffrey stopped the car and pulled over and switched on the overhead map-light and without a word put his hand out for the A to Z; how he turned over a few pages and studied them and then handed me back the book and extinguished the light and moved slowly off again into the traffic. I thought of the hundreds of other occasions when things had gone badly for us in the car. I thought of how, somehow, the between-car-journeys bit of our life suddenly became an unimaginably distant thing; I thought of how every single time it happened, my heart shrivelled up into a tiny dry peanut without the tiniest drop of love left inside it for Geoffrey, until the only thing left to do was to show him the back of my head and stare out of the window on my side and cry and silently repeat the chant, *I hate you Geoffrey Parker, I hate you, I hate you, I hate you.*

Next to the fire, the Cossack stared sadly at the body of his dead wife. Pyotr had fetched a mop and was dabbing gently at the wet floorboards around her where the ice from her clothes had begun to thaw.

Upstairs in the dormitory the bunk beds creaked. People were getting up. Soon they would be down, the young lawyer on his way to Vladivostok and the old salesmen from Irkutsk and the others, wanting their breakfast. Well, I would make breakfast. I would fill the samovar and give them hot tea and fresh rolls. I would send Pyotr into town for the carpenter and the priest and when he got back I would say to him that I was very sorry but I was going back to Birmingham now. I would tell him that he could keep the inn if he wanted it, I would leave everything for him, the beds and the cooking pots, the crockery, the vodka jugs, the knives and forks, the wood pile in the back, my balalaika, and then I would pack my bags. I would walk out into the snow and climb on the first train that was heading west out of Siberia and I would keep going until I got back to Geoffrey, and once I was there I would do what I should have done years ago, I would have some driving lessons, and when I passed my test, I would drive, and Geoffrey would navigate. And if I failed my driving test, I would take Geoffrey's hands in mine and tell him

I loved him. I would make us a good dinner and open a bottle of wine, I would put on the blue Margaret Howell linen blouse he gave me for our twelfth wedding anniversary and the cedar-wood bracelet he gave me for our fifth, and I would talk to him about public transport.

Morowa Yejidé

Tokyo Chocolate

The train leaving Nishifunabashi station is packed- a tin can of sardines. Cackling teenagers cram the perimeter. Old women haunt the end-seats, ready to fight, daring anyone to crush meticulously assembled grocery bags, or disturb a strand on their blue-tinted hair. Exhausted office assistants dot the school of people, pink and plum scarves conscientiously tied around their thin necks. Wilted businessmen wrestle sleepiness, gravity pulling at the bags under their eyes. The train roars across the water to suburban gardens and murals in Chiba, the Tokyo skyline grudgingly disappearing, damning them all for escaping its grip.

Trina is standing in the middle of the boxcar, heaved between black Armani suits and the hard edges of Prada bags. And since there are not enough handles overhead to maintain her balance, she must depend, reluctantly, on the chest cavities of three people eclipsing her personal space. She is tall, and shoots above the mass of black hair, a steeple in a field. As the boxcar shakes, through the bedrock of homogeneity, Trina's big eyes and Afro hit the crowd like seismic shock waves. Her skin crisps golden brown under their stares, incessant glances crawling over her like red ants.

But the end is near, Trina thinks, tomorrow in fact being graduation day, though the idea circles her head like smoke, its final meaning just beyond her grasp. And she is not sure what the finished painting of her stay in Japan will look like, what she will see when she stands back and contemplates the strokes and shades in all their entirety. On days of extreme exhaustion, such as this one, she misses anonymity, longs for the cold, uninterested eyes of Washingtonians. And yet, standing in her blatant state, Trina is clandestine, an agent out in the open, yet cloaked in mystery.

Two businessmen, waterlogged from rounds of sake, discuss the stranger. "Where do you think she's from?" one asks, gawking, a smile spreading across his flushed face. He is secure in his drunkenness, ensconced in island mentalities, sure that the foreigner cannot understand a word he is saying.

The other man shrugs. Molecules of his smelly breath snake around them. His head bobs as he snaps to an imagined song, jaundiced eyes raking over the anomaly. "Maybe Africa? Like Nigeria? Nah, probably not. Most of these blacks come here from America."

Trina imagines him awkwardly dancing on the stage of a karaoke bar in Ginza, rap video vixens gyrating behind him on a fifty-two inch screen.

Belching, the inquisitor leans even closer to the specimen, studying dark crystal. "She might be a model," he says.

Trina smirks behind an emotionless face.

His buddy snickers, voice dropping an octave. "Ask

her. I dare you to ask her."

Dragon breath shakes his head. "It's no good. My English is no good."

"Do it," the other snarls.

Trina thinks about allowing them to go on, while everyone is pretending not to be listening. But she pauses in the blackness of stealth, a desire to stun them growing in the crevice of her bra. All these long days she has kept silent. She has learned the weight of custom and restraint, and how words spoken too quickly sink to unknown depths. But couldn't she say something just once? Say it. "I'm an exchange student at Waseda," she quips in Japanese, instantly becoming holy. Only children born on beds of emerald ivy go to Waseda University. They swing eight-foot Kendo poles on black volcanic sands, the Japan Sea crashing behind them. They are the alchemists of tea ceremonies, a shower of pink cherry blossom petals kissing their shoulders. They are the anointed, seated squarely on the maroon leather seats of parliament, confident half-smiles dressing their faces.

At Trina's words, the businessmen are aghast, suffocating, their minds trying unsuccessfully to reconcile the holy with what is standing before them. And there is nothing left in their Lucky cigarette-choked lungs to reply beyond, "Eh?" And they look down because, of course, there is no room to back away, no point of egress for at least four minutes and thirty-eight long seconds. And even the bickering and yammering of the teenagers has crashed to a halt, a bushy-haired boy stopping mid-sentence. The atmosphere has thickened into cement, crushing the can into silence and disbelief, the boxcar reeling from the fallout of Trina's utterance. In the arrested din, Trina listens to the howling wind rattling the loose window slats, catching a glimpse of Tokyo Disney World across the bay, the lighted Ferris wheel twinkling.

The old women guarding the exits suck their teeth, grumbling about the poor example the men have set for the alien. One blue top admonishes the inebriated with an icy glare. "Crying shame," she says, straightening the leg folds of her dress to their original severe crease. At the next stop the dispossessed quickly tumble out of the smeared doors. As the train rolls by the platform, Trina watches them through the window, shaking their heads, gesticulating wildly.

But now, in addition to the watchtower from which her looks announce themselves, Trina is something even more inexplicable. The office assistants look at her, gripping the straps of their purses, betrayal burning their pupils. Mama-san, Trina's host mother, tells her Japanese people like special things. You are special, Mama-san says, in their long afternoon conversations. Trina clings to her words, her cover voluntarily blown. Closing her eyes, she thinks of the Blue Mountains of Hakuba she visited over Spring break, how crescent moons sailed indigo skies and rainbows arched lakes after rain. The train jerks, and she thinks of the pickaninny dolls in the gift shop at the Hakuba visitor's lodge, their protruding eyes begging for deliverance from key chains and stickers.

A sickeningly sweet voice cuts through the squeaking of steel on tracks. "Makuhari Hongo," chimes the automated attendant. As the train slows, she chatters politely, incessantly, warning of the dangers of not watching one's step, her pleas to collect umbrellas and newspapers dipped in syrup. Trina empties onto the platform with the throng of others and heads for her bicycle parked below. Mounting, her body cooling from the burn of the spotlight, she is thankful for the cover of darkness en route to her host family's house. Her stomach grumbles furiously at the smells of restaurants nearby. Weight gain is unthinkable in Tokyo, the body on constant watch for enough calories to make it through the day.

Trina cycles quickly through quaint, tree-lined roads, delighting in the fresh air of late evening, skidding to the last house on a charming dead-end street. It is a beautiful home, carefully built near a natural spring well, the water jetting from the sweating kitchen faucet breathtakingly delicious. There is a pretty Zenish garden out back, and on clear, quiet days she can smell the Makuhari Sound and glimpse Mount Fuji far, far away.

"Tadaima," Trina tolls at the front door, hurriedly kicking off her shoes and sliding into slippers.

Mama-san awaits her at the dining room table. She is sprite, well into the golden years, her plump cheeks flanking a pouty smile. On Tuesdays and Thursdays she swims at the local community center, after which she counsels young neighborhood mothers. 'New mothers sometimes need help with things and understanding what needs to be done,' Mama-san tells Trina, patriotic responsibility edging her proclamation. Trina dumps her heavy bag in the corner and collapses into the dining room chair. They begin a ritual, one of many.

"How was class today?" Mama-san says, knowing the question is colorless now, but unwilling to part with the habit of asking. She sits a cup in front of Trina and fills it with green tea. "Drink just a little," she says, as she always instructs Trina in the evening because the tea is laced with caffeine. Mama-san settles into her seat, smiling, ready to hear the details of her ward's day.

Trina takes a few sips, melting as it slides down her throat. She is amazed to be graduating tomorrow, her experience a kaleidoscope of impression and memory. "Class was good. Everyone's excited about the ceremony," she says. The table is decorated with snacks of all kinds. She rips into sheets of dried seaweed and shrimp-flavored crackers. "Can't believe it's finally here," she says, crunching.

Mama-san looks at her, rolling the tape in her mind back to the first day when she wondered how they'd get along. In her house. Eating her food. With no English. At the university orientation, the other host mothers had looked at the pair standing together in the green quad sympathetically, nodding their heads, offering salutations of good luck and best wishes framed in dread, all of them unprepared for anything more exotic than blond hair. But since those awkward first days, Mama-san's pride in Trina has plumed into peacock splendor, though she looks upon it only in the twilight of her private thoughts.

Mama-san thinks of all the times she led Trina through the labyrinth of her studies, how together they decrypted nuance and ground through the substratum of innuendo, how they stood on the cliffs of the meaning of things, gazing into the blue. She thinks of how she has stopped worrying about whether the rice is washed and ready in the cooker for the next day's meal, since Trina does this without being asked, and how she has come to instinctively include Trina's favorites on the grocery list. In the backwaters of her mind, she has woven a lively home again.

And when the old woman thinks of Trina's graduation tomorrow, she is reminded of the cruelty of brevity. In her long years, she has come to know its spiteful hand, how it cuts through delicate vines pains-takingly strung, slashing what is cherished without deference. And she has grown less sure if there really is a beginning within an ending, as the proverbs and fables of her youth have told her. And a shadow descends on her when she thinks of tomorrow, something she isn't proud of. "You've done well," Mama-san says, cracking open a container of warmed tofu squares. "Eat more," she urges, setting a plate and spice shaker in front of Trina.

And there is a hollow sound in Mama-san's voice that Trina has never heard before, but dismisses as the fatigue of old age. Trina looks at the shaker of hot spice, thinking of Papa-san. Piri Piri he calls it, for the sound it makes when it is sprinkled, turning everything it touches into soul food. On the rare occasions Papa-san is home at a decent hour, the two of them sit at the table together in lovely silence, grinning and chewing. Thinking of him, Trina picks up the shaker and seasons the tofu heavily.

"Papa-san won't be too much longer," Mama-san tells Trina. They both know this is a lie. Mama-san will be sitting there until well after midnight awaiting her husband, when he will hobble into the living room, dizzy from ten hours of supervising his staff and three more hours of showmanship over cocktails.

Trina glances at the empty adjoining living room, straining to hear activity upstairs. Nothing. "Where is Mariko?" she asks.

A long silence. Venetian blinds roll down Mama-san's face, closing sharply into a white facade. "She's not home yet," she says.

"Oh," Trina says, feeling guilty again for asking. Mariko had dropped out of high school, was not in college, as her parents felt she should have been, and spent the better part of her time reveling in postmodern nihilism. 'I'm not going to marry,' she likes to say when they browse fashion magazines on her bedroom floor. She is a beautiful girl by most standards, and thinks that should be sufficient for all she might end up doing in life. 'I'm sick of that shit about everything being over, if you don't marry by twenty-four,' she often says. She is probably out partying right now, Trina thinks, and Papa-san will end up sending Mama-san to bed in the witching hours while he keeps watch for her to come home.

"Nine o'clock," Mama-san announces, the blinds lifting, her voice returning to its soothing gurgle. Mariko's storm cloud has passed over, temporarily, and she gets up to turn on the news. A severe looking man is reporting rapid fire about student protests at a university in Seoul. The news cuts to footage of students clashing with police, smoke bombs and flaming bottles flying through the air.

"Those Koreans are always fighting," says Mama-san. "Their hearts have always been too quick to anger, you know. And there's so much heat in their diet, what with all the Kimchi and strong flavors on everything," she says, sighing heavily. "It's not healthy. Keeps the blood pressure up." She shakes her head and pours herself another cup of tea. "That's why," she says, eyeing the Piri Piri, "we Japanese don't eat too much peppers and such. Our diet is basically plain, you know."

Trina chopsticks another mouthful of tofu, thinking about their weekend family trip to the Japanese National Museum in Ueno Park (Mariko wasn't there). She and Papa-san had stood on the gleaming marble, looking at a tenth century special exhibit of ancient Korea.

A prehistoric map of the Asian continent hung behind a row of colorful attire like a papyrus, the Japanese islands drifting on the Pacific Ocean. 'This garb looks like the kimonos,' Trina said in wonder. Papa-san was quiet for a moment. 'Well, they should,' he said, running a hand over his balding head. Mama-san had moved on to the Ainu masks without saying a word.

Trina looks at Mama-san and grabs the remote. "Isn't Tokyo Love Story on now?" she asks. It's a decidedly silly show; full of tearful women named Yuki and the furrowed brows of men forever misunderstood. But the dialogue runs at an easygoing clip, the melodrama entertaining in a mind-numbing sort of way. Mariko and Trina sometimes giggle through the show together with tall glasses of iced Oolong. Trina watches for fullness. Mariko watches for emptiness.

Mama-san gives Trina a look. "Maybe," she says, which means she would prefer she not turn it on. Trina flips through the channels, passing Tokyo Love Story, pausing on a medical channel. A baby has just been born and screams heartily when the doctor holds him up. Half listening, Trina catches the narrator say, "Koku-jin," meaning black person. After the first few days of life, the now pale baby's skin will begin to change color, turning brown....

"Really?" Mama-san exclaims, looking at Trina incredulously. For her, there is no end to the wonders of black people, and she relishes this kind of chance encounter with astonishing bits of information.

When the two of them sit down for their Sunday afternoon ritual of tea and sweets, they exchange comments and questions until dinner. Last Sunday, after months of getting up her nerve, Trina asked Mama-san what she thought about Hiroshima. Mama-san stared at the cocoa powder atop the slices of Tiramisu for a long time without saying anything. She is from a southern prefecture, the youngest daughter of a traditional kimono-making family. She is of the generation that has lived both during the happening and afterwards.

In the long silence, Trina was a bit ashamed of her curiosity, but it had been tugging at her since she hit the ground at Narita Airport. 'Papa-san said the American soldiers used to give out Hershey's chocolate bars to the children during the occupation,' she offered weakly, fidgeting in the old woman's muteness.

Mama-san put another slice of Tiramisu on their pastry plates without looking at Trina. It was a question she had expected eventually, but the heaviness of it took her breath nonetheless. 'I was a little thing, but what I remember the most were the holes,' she said at last. 'Where my cousin was, when we finally did go out to see where she might have been, they told us the women ran further into the countryside, that they had tried frantically to find cover, digging holes to put their children in the ground. Trying to protect them from the beast that had killed even the Lightning God, they said.' Her face tightened. 'The grass was still white, and there were holes everywhere,' she said. After that, Mama-san and Trina sat quietly together for a long time, staring out into the ocean of things they found difficult to understand.

The narrator on the television show continued about craniums and birth weights.

"Really?" Mama-san asks Trina again, louder.

"Really," Trina says.

"Incredible," Mama-san says, taking in the thought. "But some of you are darker and some are lighter, huh?"

Trina thinks about engaging her in the other layers: ice ages and geography; the horrors of plantation life; race mixing; recessive genes; high-yellow fixations and that sort of thing. But she is stuffed. "That's true," she says.

They look at each other. And Trina is certain that the old woman can tell from her tone and the shine in her eyes that there is so much more to the story, but that she does not have, or is unwilling to expend, the energy to drill down through history and pain. It is a conversation for Sundays, and they agree on this without saying so.

"Why don't you get some rest?" Mama-san says, more a command than a request.

The chair feels stiff now, and Trina is ready to stretch out, but not ready to go to bed. She puts down the remote and wanders to the couch, sinking into its plush leather.

"Grab a pillow," says Mama-san, pointing to a stack of silk-embroidered cushions on the floor by the bookcase.

Trina lumbers over and picks out a green one, pulling the stack forward. There are photo albums on the bottom shelf behind the pillows. "Can I look at these?" she asks.

Mama-san is engrossed in medical terminology. "Look at what?"

Trina picks up a few dusty albums, showing the faded covers. "These."

"Sure," says Mama-san.

Trina settles into the couch with a throw blanket over her lap, flipping through the pages. There are pictures of porcelain-faced women wrapped in elaborate kimonos adorned with butterflies. There are scenes of Mama-san and Papa-san smiling in front of temples, Mariko's cherub face staring from a stroller next to them. Trina comes to a picture that she thinks is Mariko, but realizes is Mama-san as a young woman, her eyes electric, beaming through the cracked plastic sheets. "When was this?"

Mama-san yawns. "Huh?"

"How old were you when this was taken?" Trina asks.

Mama-san comes over to the couch and sits next to Trina. As she stares at the picture, her face is illuminated from a light not in the room, the low current in her eyes intensifying. "Ah. Yes, that was me, wasn't it? Twenty I think, about your age. My modeling days."

Trina tries to fathom how a woman who orders the items in her cupboard alphabetically and keeps a petty cash envelope in the credenza could ever have done anything as orchid-like as modeling. "Really?" she asks.

Mama-san's unspoken thoughts settle over them, mixing with the dust. "Trina, whatever it is you decide you want to do, make sure you do it," she says, rising. She points to a little ship entombed in a bottle on the end table, and says, "Remember the boat." The old woman returns to the television, leaving a trail of echoes. And Trina remembers Mama-san saying one Sunday that sometimes life can be like that boat in the bottle, that once a thing is constructed, and all of its pieces are brought to their end, it becomes only what it is.

The cat scratching Trina's bedroom door awakens her in the morning light of Graduation Day. She hears the clinking of dishes and silverware downstairs, the sports report on the television in full swing. She goes down the hallway, pausing at Mariko's door. A radio is playing whimsical songs, indicating she has made it home at some hour in the night. Trina pads down the steps with anticipation, wondering how the day will unfold.

The dining room table is decked in majesty, food of all sorts punctuated with opulent bowls and the chrysanthemums of hand painted plates. In the center of the table there is a box wrapped in silver paper, topped with a brilliant red bow.

Papa-san comes in from the kitchen. "Oh, so you're up." He pours them both a cup of tea, his smile a bit nervous.

Trina does not notice this and she is lost in the spectacular display. "This is just lovely. Look at all this!"

Papa-san sits down, motioning for Trina to join him. "Mama-san did put on a show, didn't she?" he says.

And it is only then, looking around and hearing nothing but the television, that Trina notices the absence of something that is almost an appendage of the dining room. "Where is she? The post office? The market square? I thought she said something about us all going out later, after the ceremony."

"No," Papa-san says, looking away. "She's not going."

"The square?"

"The ceremony."

A long silence. And Trina cannot believe what she is hearing, cannot understand why Mama-san would not wish to see this event, a culmination of something she had so much of a hand in making. Disappointment routs her throat, and she is only able to manage one word. "Why?"

"It's difficult," says Papa-san. "Sometimes," he says slowly, staring at the green leaves drowned at the bottom of his cup, "we don't want to see a thing end." He looks as if he wants to say something else, but folds it up and puts it away.

The two of them float quietly at the table, and Trina distracts herself with thoughts of plane tickets, of the boy she hopes will be waiting for her when she comes out of the gate, of Redskins and pumpkin pie, of white monuments and the black Potomac River. And when this falls away, she thinks of all of the afternoons she walked moonscapes with Mama-san, looking into craters full of surprises and realizations. And she thinks of all the species of roses in the garden of their friendship that they, after her leaving, will not have the opportunity to examine and discuss. All of it gone.

"But I'll be there," says Papa-san, trying mightily to smile, knowing Mama-san has gone to the murky waters of the sound to think about things they no longer discuss, knowing Mariko will remain in bed. He picks up the box and hands it to Trina. "She wanted you to have this."

Trina tries to share in Papa-san's feigned cheer, nodding and smiling, saying thank you profusely. She opens the gift, an extravagant assortment of chocolates with a card inside. Mama-san's elegant calligraphy dances across the ivory. "For your other Sundays," Trina reads, bursting into tears.

Nick Holdstock

Amy

One night, a few months ago, I went into my flat-mate's room. I put back the pillow and then, without thinking, bent down and pulled out one of the plastic trays that slot under her bed. In the first were trousers, t-shirts and shorts, so I pushed it back in, and pulled out the other. In that one there were bras and pants so I brought a black pair to my nose and slowly, deeply, breathed.

I had taken the pillow because a friend was sup-posed to be staying. When I'd finally made up the spare bed— the duvet cover was a nightmare —I realised there was no pillow and so earlier that day I'd gone into Amy's room. I didn't think she would mind: she was in Romania with her adventurous boyfriend.

I remember listening outside while the floorboards creaked. If she had somehow been inside— having re-turned from her holiday early after breaking-up with Tim —it would have seemed strange, almost creepy, for me to be stood there so long, as if I was waiting for a hole, or crack, to open in the wood.

I pushed the door with my knuckles. It swung in with an unfortunate groan but no one said Get out. I went in and took a pillow, then paused for a quick look round (although she'd lived there eight months, I'd only been in once before, when I had stood and watched while she wrote me a cheque). I saw that the bookcase was full, that she had a thriving yucca and a Vettriano print. I certainly didn't think about touching the trays under the bed.

When I returned the pillow later (my friend had inexplicably decided to stay in a Travel Lodge) I was pretty drunk. When I brought her pants to my nose, it was mostly as a joke; there's something unavoidably comic about sniffing someone's underwear. My thoughts during the three or four seconds that I smelt the spring freshness of the fabric conditioner, felt the softness of the crotch (which although far from worn, felt too thin to be new) were anything but erotic. I smelt them the way you breathe in a rose on your way to the bus stop. At no point did I imagine Amy taking off these pants, slowly, or with a jerk of eloquent impatience.

Although Amy wasn't ugly, she wasn't particularly hot. She had a big head. She limped. But on the morning when she came to view the place— her long curls were heavy with rain, she had not dressed for the weather —I was instantly aware that she could be attractive. Her features were very symmetrical; her nose was slightly upturned. Despite the limp she had a way of walking that made almost no sound. As we moved between the lounge and the kitchen I asked what she did. She said she worked in a department store. In the Ladies section.

After our first morning I never thought of Amy in anything but a platonic fashion, and certainly never wondered what kind of pants she wore. She wasn't the first girl I'd lived with. At university I'd shared a house with Celine, from Bruges, who had a big nose, and Anna, from Krakow, who played the trumpet, and then, after my parents died and I bought this flat, there was Greta, from Hamburg, and Myrto, from Thebes, and although I got on well with them, there was never any question of anything happening between us— not even when Anna came into my room one night and lay down next to me. Although I said her name several times she did not reply, or move, and after a while I got up and went to the sofa. It seemed too big a risk to get involved with my flatmate. After I'd bought the flat there was also the sense that, as landlord, it would be irresponsible for me to do anything, which is not to say that they looked up to me, or that I thought of myself as some kind of authority figure, just that there was a difference in our situations. On the very few occasions I went into their rooms to carry out some essential act of maintenance, I paid absolutely no attention to either the small, white pants with blue polka dots Greta left on her floor (she was the least tidy German person I have ever met) or to the large, red bras Myrto hung from a hook.

Even the smell of Amy's pants wasn't that arousing. After a minute I put them back and went to bed. When I woke up next morning it wasn't the first thing I thought of. I had breakfast, showered, read the paper and it was only when the post came that I remembered my actions of the night before. I could have gone straight to her room. As far as I knew, she was still in the Carpathians, climbing and hiking and camping with good old adventurous Tim. I didn't even think of her pants until very late that night, after I'd had dinner and watched *The Unbearable Lightness of Being*. I thought of the lace, the soft gusset, and after I went and cleaned my teeth, I stood outside her room and listened. I tried to think of a plausible explanation for going in, something I could casually blurt if in fact she was sleeping or lying on the bed in her most excellent pants.

I was still trying to think of an excuse when I pushed open the door. I went to the bed and pulled out the tray. I lifted up the black pair and examined the rest. Most of them were plain, simple colours, blue and green, apart from a very pretty pair that did up with small pink bows. I looked closely at these because they reminded me of a pair my ex-girlfriend had; sometimes, if she thought I'd been good, she'd wander through her flat in these while her cat, who never liked me, made noises of feline confusion as it followed her round. She treated it like a performance, and for her it definitely was. She thought she had a gift for the dramatic, but if she did, I'm sad to say, it was a meagre one that wasn't at all well-wrapped. But we'd still had a wonderful six weeks, and although there were obviously problems, I thought we'd work them out. I certainly didn't expect her to end it so abruptly. She wrote me a long, unpleasant letter that was rather upsetting. After I read it I went and stood by the river, feeling bad and watching swans that looked incredibly soft.

And as I held Amy's pants I felt the same sadness. I had to hold the black pair to my face to stop myself from crying. Kneeling there by Amy's bed, with her black pants against my face, I suppose I can be forgiven for having certain thoughts about her, mainly to do with her wearing these black pants while on a beach in

Greece. And yes, I *did* become aroused, but I didn't do anything about it there. Instead I took the pants into my room. I opened a catalogue to a marked page, and then, whilst looking at girls in bikinis (none of whom resembled Amy), I began to enjoy myself, and the feeling got better and better, and sometimes the pants were against my face, and sometimes they were by my side, but I was always very careful to keep them away from my groin. Afterwards I made sure my hands were clean before checking the pants. There were no traces or hairs and I put them back in Amy's room then quickly fell asleep.

Amy came back three days later. I was almost asleep when I heard the key in the lock, then the sound of her putting down bags, switching her light on. I lay in the darkness, wondering if she would suddenly shout, and although I was worried, I also felt surprised. I hadn't expected to feel this way: after four nights of going into her room, three of coming back into mine, the whole thing had started to feel routine, something I did after brushing my teeth as part of getting ready for bed. I lay there a long time, well after her sounds had finished, waiting for her fist to bang into my door.

Next day was Sunday. As usual, I sat in the front room with a thick wedge of newspaper. I read the main section, then the Review, then the Business section that was very dull. I was halfway through Lifestyle when I heard Amy close the bathroom door. Next there was the sound of water and before I knew it I was thinking of her in the shower in the little black pants. And this was not something I wanted to think about, because as I said, I have always had a rule about not being attracted to my flatmates.

I read the Travel section, then the Personals. When

I heard the water stop I put the paper down. I stood in the light of morning while cars droned outside. When I heard the bolt slide back I walked into the hall. Her dressing gown was thin, and new; her hair was wrapped in a small towel that looked like a bandage. "Hey," I said, and she said "Hey," and it shouldn't have been uncomfortable because we had seen each other coming out of the shower before. But I was worried she somehow knew, because even when you're trying to be careful, you can make a mistake. But the awkwardness was all mine, because when I stammeringly asked if she'd had a good trip, Amy smiled and said yes. She shut her door neither quickly, as if she were anxious, or in a slow, incomplete fashion suggesting not only reluctance, but also a sense that the whole business of imposing a solid barrier between the soon-to be-naked-you and your flatmate/landlord is only a tiresome act demanded by a bourgeois sense of so-called decency, and that actually if he did see his flatmate/tenant removing her robe and slowly pulling on a small pair of clean black pants it would not mean anything in particular or be, in any sense, a 'big deal' to him, the flatmate/landlord, or to her, the flatmate/tenant, partly because they had seen naked people before (he, the flatmate/landlord), and been seen naked before (she, the flatmate/tenant), but mostly because they had a good relationship whose platonic boundaries had been respectfully defined during their eight months happily living together.

I stood looking at her door and then I went into the bathroom. It was full of the smell of her shampoo, which was the smell of apples, and it didn't matter that it wasn't real apples I was smelling, but instead the aroma caused by certain synthetic compounds whose sole purpose was to mimic the real thing to such an extent that my weak olfactory sense was confused (and in some sense, tricked) into thinking it was enjoying one thing when actually it was taking pleasure from something else. I shut the door and breathed in deeply; took off my clothes, turned on the shower, stood under the hot, fast water.

Amy was home a lot over the next few weeks. There must have been nights when she was at Tim's, but I was never sure of this till after the fact. Tim came over a few times and although we'd got on fine before, I found myself making more of an effort, asking him how his research was going— he was in his second year of a PhD in Sports Psychology, something to do with mental images while throwing the javelin —and once or twice we shared a beer while he talked about football. I'm not suggesting we became friends, just that we were friendly. Of course, all our chats ended the same way: he went into Amy's room and then the door was shut.

Things were also different with Amy. I made a real effort not to think of her limping round in only a pair of pants. I banished thoughts of a long modelling session, (my reward for being 'good') during which I'd sit on a hard chair under the Vettriano while she put on every item in the plastic tray. First a plain blue pair, which I'd watch move back and forth, until she stopped and offered a questioning look, to which my only response would be an almost-brusque shake of the head. Then she would walk behind a screen printed with butterflies, pagodas and other Japanese motifs, and after a pause, during which I could only imagine her removing the rejected item, she would reappear wearing a different item, which I would sit and watch as she paraded to the far wall and back. I would reject this in the same

fashion, and then she'd go behind the screen and re-
move this pair, and then she'd reappear with another
pair that I'd also reject. She'd put them all on, but I'd
shake my head, even at the pretty pair with the pink
bows. After these she'd walk to the screen and then
there'd be the usual pause, except she'd not come out. I
would begin to worry that this last refusal, of what were
surely charming pants, had in some way offended her,
and I would wonder whether to call out something en-
couraging, or if I should just say modesty-be-damned
and go behind the screen. After a long debate, I would
stand, and prepare to go over, and then Amy would
come out from behind the screen wearing the black pair
that I had not seen, touched or smelled since she got
back from the mountains and walk slowly towards me
till I was smelling the clean and wholesome aroma I
could never get my own clothes or towels to have, no
matter how much fabric conditioner I put in the machine.

During the first few weeks this scene replayed in my
mind. Obviously, it made things difficult, but eventually
I got to the point where I had these thoughts in the
morning, after lunch, once or twice in the evening;
apart from these times she was just my old flatmate
whose pants I'd never smelt. When we spoke of the
weather, of the bills that needed paying, it usually struck
me, with singular force, just how much I liked her, and
not because of her pants, but because she, Amy Der-
showitz, was part of that endangered species known as
the Really Nice. She was kind, patient, clean (she never
left her washing up; her room was always spotless); she
always paid her rent on time, she never played her music too loud: she was, in many ways, the ideal
flatmate/tenant, and there were many times that I

stopped what I was doing and thought of her (and not in the manner described above) and realised how lucky how I was to have her as a flatmate/tenant.

I tried to make more of an effort. I bought flowers for the kitchen. I bought new curtains for her room. When she came home from a long day at work there was a note on the kitchen table telling her to eat some of my ratatouille because I'd cooked too much. Which she did, because she loved aubergine, and when I came down next morning there was a short note that I still have. It says, "Thanks very much. It was delicious! See you tonight. Amy."

It's easy to say that all this— the flowers, the food, the Krupps espresso machine I bought even though I hate coffee —was a well-disguised attempt at courtship. But this wasn't my intention, I was only trying to be nice, and besides, she was still firmly with Tim (they had just got engaged), so much so that I kept expecting her to knock on my door, look slightly shame-faced, then ask if she could come in. I would say yes, and she would come sit on the bed even though there was a chair free, and then she would say she was sorry but she was going to have to move out and I would say I too was extremely sorry and then we would look at everything except each other and I would feel very close to tears and although I wasn't looking at her, I would know that she was too, and there would be a long silence until she would say my name and that she was very sorry, and I'd say Me too. Then she'd finally start to sob and I'd have to move close to her so I could comfort her. And the whole thing would finally make me so upset that *I* would start to cry and then she'd have to be the one to comfort me.

Thankfully, this didn't happen. If anything Amy

seemed more settled— she started leaving her door open, so whenever I walked by I could see her at her desk or on the bed and there were times when *she* would cook too much and leave a note for me, a gesture which I found so touching that I always ate a plate of whatever she'd attempted to cook. There was an occasion when I'd come home just as she was scraping the non-burnt portions of pie from the dish. She was wearing a pair of rust-coloured trousers that were very wide and flapping without being flares. She turned off the hob and passed me a plate and then, as if we ate together every night, she sat down opposite me and began to eat. I chewed and chewed until I managed to swallow. Then I asked her how work was going, and she said it was going fine, and then there was a little pause because she couldn't ask me the same (I haven't had a job since I was fifteen, and that was purely an act of rebellion) but the gap in our conversation was by no means awkward or uncomfortable. I offered to open a bottle of wine. She looked confused, and I didn't insist because it had only been a spontaneous thought I happened to have spoken. It was as I raised my glass of water that she said actually, she *would* like some wine. I opened a bottle of something French and we sat and drank and as I poured her a second glass I asked if her and Tim had chosen a date. There was a significant pause before she said no, they hadn't, and I said, without a pause, that there was obviously no rush, and she took a sip, and I took a sip, and maybe she put down her glass and stood up and hooked her thumbs inside her trousers and then, without unzipping, or unbuttoning, somehow managed to drag her trousers far enough down for gravity to complete the job, and maybe she stepped out of them as if they were a costume she had worn only for a bet and now that the wager was won, the laugh had been had, it was time to return to her actual, natural form in all its remarkable beauty. And there was nothing surprising about this; it was as if I'd known that this, though not inevitable, was so very likely to happen that had it in fact *not* happened, that would probably, on balance, have been the greater surprise.

"Would you like more pie?" said Amy, even though I hadn't finished the first piece. "Yes," I said and so she slid the spatula perfectly under the pie and put it on my plate and I said thank you and filled my mouth with the remains of the first piece. And it was a small piece of bone, not that difficult to swallow, but she must have seen alarm in my eyes because she asked, with touching concern, whether I was alright, and I could not reply, because of the bone, the shock of its hardness, and then she looked away and quietly said she really didn't know; she wasn't sure; perhaps it was too soon. And as the bone scraped its way down I still did not reply and she just shook her head.

This is definitely what happened. I'm also certain that when I next saw Tim he did not stop or slow when I said hi to him. He simply lifted his head and nodded as he entered Amy's room. The door was shut, and stayed that way, and once or twice he raised his voice when he said Amy's name. It was almost three o'clock when I heard her door open and the front door slam. I don't know what their problems were, but after a year and a half together, there must have been some. Amy never gave a reason; all she said, as we lay there, was that it couldn't work. It was probably something sexual; no matter how hard I listened, no mater how long or quietly I sat, I never heard anything after her lights went out. Maybe good old mountain-climbing Tim made impossible demands. Maybe he was one of those men who think they always deserve penetrative sex. There's really no way of knowing, and I don't suppose it matters. *Something* must have been wrong. I guess it just goes to show: there's no way to tell how things stand between people.

Amy stayed in her room for most of the next week. We did not see or speak to each other, but I knew what was wrong, and therefore I did my best to make things as easy as possible for her. Every night, I cooked too much, and every night I left a note, and sometimes she ate some and sometimes she did not. I heard her phone ring a lot and most of the time it went unanswered even when she was in. Then the house phone would ring and because we did not have an answer machine it would ring and ring and ring until Tim gave up, usually after a minute or two, but there was one occasion when I *did* pick up the phone, because I hadn't heard her mobile ring, and after a pause, during which he must have lurched from surprise to relief and then to anger, he screamed, or maybe shouted, "Why won't you talk to me? I just don't under*stand*." I did not know how to respond, and so I gently put the receiver down and turned the bell off (and did not turn it back on for weeks, not until after she'd left). And now of course I understand why Tim was so confused. Even when things seem perfect, it can all come down.

The sun was burning in the room when I saw Amy next. I heard her come in, but kept my eyes closed, because I felt that seeing would dilute the incredible sense of warmth and health that the sun was creating. And she could obviously tell that this was not an ordinary moment because she didn't speak or make any noise after the initial sounds of her feet on the smooth wooden floor. And the sun was so strong that even if I *had* opened my eyes I probably wouldn't have been able to see her. In one moment I was sitting in the chair, in the light, and there were no auditory signs that Amy was still in the room. Then, with no sense of transition, there was the sound of fabric moving against itself and then something stroked my cheek, something like the long sash of a dressing gown that has just been undone so the robe can open. I put my hands in front of me and my fingers met lace and it was then, or sometime later, that I stopped being Amy's landlord and became her friend.

It can be very difficult when you get what you want. I was afraid. What if we made a mess of things? What if my longstanding reluctance was in essence correct? But it was too late. Although things were moving slowly— Amy said she wasn't ready —they could not roll back. We kissed, held hands, and sometimes lay down, but our clothes stayed on. And it was wonderful to hold her, to push my nose in her clean hair, but by the third day I was feeling impatient. When I suggested she undo her trousers, Amy misunderstood. "I thought we agreed," she said. And I could not explain. I had to apologise. Because she wouldn't have cared about context; she wouldn't have listened that long.

But although things were moving slowly, we were definitely a couple. We shopped together, ate together, every night we watched TV, her big head against my shoulder, until, around half eleven, she would yawn and then kiss me and I would pull her body to mine and put my hand on her breast and then we would grapple and grope until she said Goodnight. After this she'd go to her room and I would sit on the sofa, aroused, wondering if she was waiting for me to do what I'd promised not to. There were many occasions when I thought I'd have to pull out the drawers that slotted so perfectly under her bed, but I didn't, even when she was out, because I had much more to lose, and so the drawers stayed under the bed and every night we groped on the sofa until she said Goodnight. Now it all seems wonderfully innocent, but at the time it made me feel incredibly frustrated. We were doing everything else together; why could she not take off her trousers?

I don't know what I said or did. All I know is, after three weeks, she didn't say Goodnight. Instead she undid the buttons on her grey silk blouse. She arched her back, undid her bra and then my hands were dragging down the zip of her black skirt. She was wearing the wonderful black pair, as if I had asked her to, as if she'd always known. As I stroked the material my fingers shook so much that she said, "Don't worry." We kissed and she unzipped my fly and all the while my fingers rubbed her understanding pants. The smooth fabric began to get wet. "Shall I take these off?" she said, and I did not say No.

Amy slid them down and off and then I could not see them. My hands searched among the cushions but they had slipped down. "Come on," she said. "Let's go to bed." She stood and limped to her room; I followed, looking back. We lay on her bed, now naked, then she got on top of me and it felt very strange, like she was someone in a film who had walked out of the screen. She moved back and forth on me but it was not quite sex. As she took me into her mouth I thought about the pants, if they were behind the cushions, if they were on the lounge floor, and although I wasn't worried they'd be lost or stolen, I still wanted to see and hold them, just so I could be sure.

"What's wrong?" she said.

"Nothing," I said.

"Are you sure?"

"Yes, I'm just tired."

"OK," she said, and then I held her, and as she went to sleep, she twitched, but did not wake up. I waited until she was snoring. Then I slid quietly out of bed and went into the lounge.

Margot Taylor

Ebb Tide

Our mugs of tea grow cold after she tells me 'Cancer, Henry.' I can only sit, for as long as she wants me there, and wonder what she's thinking, while the rain spits and the waves slap, and the old oyster smack lifts at her mooring. A curlew calls, somewhere off over the mud-banks, and Jane says 'Listen to that.' She must have heard the sound a thousand times. But Jane will emerge to watch swans beat the water in take-off; she's first to spot a seal or the frightened scatter of fry when the mackerel come up river. She can watch the tide rise and fall without feeling there's a better way to use her time.

'I'm never going to leave Gypsy,' she says. She rummages and pulls out a vintage Dom Perignon. 'I've hung on to this for years. But I want to drink it now.'

River Gypsy, caught in an eddy, starts to swing. The oaks on the shore travel past the window, then slide back again. I fill and later refill our glasses. The wind gusts, the boat swings and tilts, the champagne tastes exquisite.

'Henry, I can't leave her,' she tells me again.

'If it came to it you could live with me,' I say, and then wish I hadn't. I might have to wash her. Feed her. There would be pain and mess. We are neighbours, not lovers. I remember there is a son, somewhere on land.

'Don't be ridiculous, Henry,' she says. 'I couldn't possibly live in that scruffy tub of yours. And anyway, it's time you went. Really went. How long have you been telling me you're off?'

She is right, I think, as I row a haphazard course back to Spray. I have stayed too long on the river. I am sick of mud at low tide, close wooded hills, two-storey ferries packed with tourists, the wash from speeding weekenders.

Spray IV is steel, a hotchpotch, modified or added to whenever I've had time in a new port or money in my pocket. She loves to sail, leaps forward at the touch of a breeze. Nothing, not even the many lovers, in many ports, has kept us from sailing, until this apathy, seeped into me from the slow river. My poor boat's ropes are green, her deck paint is flaking, weed and mussels dangle from her bottom. She has become a rank badger's sett, the bolt-hole of a lone male. To sleep I slide into a quarter berth already occupied by two damp oars, spare fenders and a toolbox. Every locker is jammed, every surface covered. If Jane moved in there wouldn't be a square inch to stow her things.

I watch as Jane's son visits and takes her to the hospital for treatment and returns her home again. I call on some days but not others. I make no offers except to shop but I buy little extras, a ripe mango or some dark chocolate. I check for the gleam of Gypsy's oil-lamps each evening. Then Ken the harbour master tells me

Jane was rushed to hospital in the night. The following day that she is stable but weak.

'Her son will be with her,' I say. 'I'll drop by soon; but I must get to work on Spray, and be off before the autumn gales.'

A week, two weeks and more go by. I drink too much tea and watch branches and bits of polystyrene float past. I hear geese overhead. It's only afterwards I realise I never saw them, but looked instead to see if Jane had stuck her head out. Then one day Gypsy is gone, her mooring empty. I call up Ken but get no reply. I tear down the river, push into the crush of tenders at the town pontoon. I hurry through streets clogged with summer visitors. Yes, they tell me at the hospital, she's here. I am shown to a thin old woman, propped on pillows.

'Haven't you gone yet? I thought you'd be halfway across Biscay by now.'

Unmistakably Jane.

'Get me out of here,' she says. 'This place is killing me.'

I find a wheelchair and wheel her down to the front. A yacht tacks out to the river mouth; Ken lifts a hand as he passes in his launch; the gulls swoop and scream. Jane is too busy taking it all in to say much. This visiting the sick seems a small, easy thing after all.

But back on the ward she's still quiet.

'Does your son visit?'

'Often enough.'

Presumably she knows Gypsy has been moved? Sold? I daren't ask. I glance around at the other sick people, reduced to tubes and blank faces and open mouths.

'Have you made friends?'

Jane doesn't bother to answer. Perhaps it was a stupid question but at least I am trying. She doesn't seem to be. She didn't mean, when she said 'get me out of here', she didn't mean out of here for good? No-one could expect that. Is she harking back to the offer I made? When I distinctly remember she turned me down. And told me I was ridiculous.

'Look out the window,' Jane says.

I see the tops of trees that do not slide past.

'You've no idea how hard it is to sleep on land,' she says. It's all so bloody solid.'

Sleeping inside a boat is like being in a giant womb. There is a constant shifting and stirring, murmuring and creaking. You are held and protected. But I don't say any of this to Jane.

I get back to Spray and look her over and make a list. I take her to town and lean her against the harbour wall. I dry her out and scrub her bottom and antifoul her. I buy new warps and check her rigging and have the sails valeted. I treat her to an anchor windlass to save my back. I stock up on non-perishables like lentils and rice and tins of corned beef. To stow them I do a big clearout of stuff I've kept for years like lengths of spare chain and an old mainsail. Back on the mooring I varnish woodwork, paint out lockers, paint her deck and hull until she gleams.

At night I take down books by my old sailing heroes and adventurers, returning again and again to Slocum, whose boat has been the namesake for every boat I've owned. Who after a lifetime of single-handed voyages disappeared at sea, presumed run down by a tanker, or hit by a whale. It's the way to go, doing what you love, no hanging about with lost faculties.

We are looking great, both of us, and feeling great,

almost ready for the off. Spray strains and snatches at her mooring. 'Patience, old girl,' I tell her. I have a picture, it is in my head all the time, of the moment when I will show her to Jane, how I will wheel Jane down to the river front and there Spray will be, looking wonderful, gleaming.

I deflate the tender and tie it on deck. I stow the sail cover. I run the engine, startling some waders which take flight from the muddy bank. I slip the mooring and Spray trickles downriver, past Gypsy's empty mooring, past a heron poised on the wooded shoreline, past the rotting barge and the boatyard with its cranes and slings. She rounds a corner and the river opens up on either side, the town plastered to the hillside, the car ferry crossing ahead of us, the rowing crews and commercial crabbers, all the regular users. From nowhere a rib tears across my bow, cutting a deep swathe. But nothing can unsettle me, for we are on our way, out of here. But first, Jane. I check for space on the town pontoon and get my shorelines ready.

'Do you see Spray?'

I shouldn't need to point. She's here, right in front of us. Jane is looking but somehow just missing. When she turns her face that's all it is. A turned face. Her grip is so tight, so claw-like on my arm I want to shake it off.

'I don't believe it,' I say. 'You can't see, can you? Why didn't you tell me?'

'When could I have done that, Henry? When exactly? Or perhaps I should've asked Ken to pass on the message.'

I want her to see Spray. I want her to be amazed. I say nothing, afraid of sounding childish.

We watch the usual busy river stuff. I watch it. After a bit Jane says 'Can I sit on her?'

'No,' I say. 'Too complicated.'

Fiddlesticks,' she says. 'You're scared.'

I push her back to the hospital. I don't tell her I'm leaving. I stump around the shops, doing my last few jobs. A shoulder whacks into me. 'Watch where you're going,' I mutter without looking up. 'Bloody people.'

I give Spray a shove, step on deck, throw the lines down in a tangled heap. I haul the main up. Cut the engine. Tug at the genoa which cracks and fills. The boat surges forward. The only sound is of waves slapping the hull.

I'm used to feeling lonely surrounded by people; but I have never felt so alone at sea before. Spray pulls on, away from the coast, and I am in utterly the wrong place. My friend Jane is stranded in a hospital bed. And I am a blind fool. Wasn't it for her I cleaned and painted the boat and emptied lockers?

'I hope she'll have us,' I say to Spray as we blow back into port.

'Henry?'

'Yes.'

'You've come.'

'Yes.'

'My grab bag,' Jane says. 'Under my bed. It has morphine, clothes, a letter from my doctor.'

The nurse helps her get dressed. I fetch a wheel-chair. A porter carries her bag and a pile of hospital pillows. When we get to the boat Jane stands and we help her on. She's so light she nearly takes off. I hold her steady, put my arms right around her. We're just standing there, filled up with standing there, when the porter taps me on the shoulder. He has the wheelchair in the cockpit for us. I thank him and say goodnight.

Jane, seated, reaches out and runs a finger along the smooth new paint.

'You've done her up beautifully,' she says.

I cast off and an ebb tide carries us swiftly away. It is almost dark and the lights have come on; the town lights reflected broad and mellow, dancing in the river, and the navigation lights burning red and green, guiding us out. Spray is barely noticed by the holidaymakers still strolling on the front. She pauses, head to wind, while I raise the main. Then she moves on, beyond the castle at the river mouth, straight out to sea.

Carol Farrelly

Ante-Purgatory

A purple backpack lies abandoned by the newspaper stand. Nobody else notices. They rush right towards the streetlights and frosted air. They surge left towards the judder of trains on tracks. Starlings swoop overhead: perhaps one of them looks down and sees the tracks that bite, like stitches, into the earth. He is blind, however, to the abandoned backpack. Only I hear the clock inside as it ticks down, muffled by a burgundy towel, speckled with yesterday's sand.

A young man reaches in, grabs the bag by its straps and sprints leftwards.

I chew again on my peppermint gum and glance at my watch.

Five minutes more until Carlotta arrives.

For fourteen years, I have kept away. Most of the others returned soon afterwards. They returned because it is the only way to reach an office door or kiss a parent's cheek or taste salt, Adriatic air again. A few, less compelled, return only on the anniversary. I have always kept away, until today.

I knew I would not cope. I do not want to hesitate at purple backpacks. I do not want to play the sniffer dog. I am afraid to turn a corner and surprise my twenty-year old ghost. The marbled, mustard-yellow walls might crack open; he would bustle towards me, green rucksack flapping against his shoulders. His eyes would gloat ambition. They would skim and glitter across me, while I stopped and stared at the most beautiful man imaginable. I could not bear it. Nobody can bear to recognise too late the beauty you never used.

The tannoy crackles. 'Si invitano i signori viaggiatori a non lasciare incustoditi i propri bagagli. I bagagli lasciati incustoditi verranno sottoposti a controllo.'

I have risked today for Charlotte. For her I brave these abattoir walls and floors. They scrub them clean, every morning. 10.26 hours, they get out their mops and surgical gloves. They make the mottled marble gleam, autumn leaves under glass. They must know: it is all a lie. You cannot stretcher away all the remains; you cannot bag and zip and shelve every trace: the greying eyelash that fell from a middle-aged man's cheek, the skinny schoolgirl's half-made handprint, the blood that trickled from a reluctant young mother's skull into the charred cement. So much blood. Poppies should grow here. Clambering, monster poppies.

My ghost is one amongst many who pick open the cracks, 10.25 every morning. He is only half a ghost. Not as angry as some.

Nobody else hears them.

A gaggle of teenagers wanders towards the exit, their trainers squeaking against the marbled floor. They do not glimpse the flapping, green rucksack. In a corner, two blonde-skinned girls stoop beneath their backpacks and peer at a map. They whisper our street names to each other in embarrassed French accents, 'Piazza Maggiore', 'Via Zamboni' and 'Via delle Belle Arti'. They do not hear the walls fall apart again. They probably know nothing of that day. Foreign and too young. Tomorrow, they will read of it in their fat guide-books and they will return, perhaps, to stare at the stopped clock outside, which juts like an ear from the wall. 10.25.

What does Charlotte know of that day? Have her eyes glittered a moment over the stopped clock? We have never spoken of it during my Saturday morning visits, when I play the diligent landlord.

The tannoy crackles again. 'Il treno delle ore 22.23 proveniente da Firenze e diretto a Venezia viaggia con un ritardo di dieci minuti.'

Another ten minutes until I can see Charlotte safe. An itch crawls up my right arm. I have waited an hour already among the collapsing mustard walls. I have sat on four benches and loitered on three platforms, trying to calm my legs whenever a Florence train arrives. I must feign coincidence if she sees me. She would misinterpret, of course.

Nine minutes more.

The train was nine minutes late that day. I would not have been there if those nine minutes had arrived on time. Others would not have been there. How many of the names would uncarve themselves from the waiting-room wall? Or if the terrorist's pale, scrubbed hands had set the timer twenty minutes later... Or if he had left the briefcase in the first-class waiting room instead of the second... I ask these questions every day. The others must also ask. Musical chairs. Why her and not him? Why you and not me? And you play their game. It creeps up on you, sometimes. You hear the music stop; you feel the rush of legs; you wonder if you deserve the cool wood of the chair-back. The people who remain standing, arms limp— paler-skinned, older, sadder—are they more deserving of death? Should you take one of their places?

Whenever I think of Charlotte, I know I should stand by the chairs. So beautiful, so deserving of safe-keeping. She would have my chair. Even if she returns with him, even if she lets his hand hold hers as she steps off the train.

Seven minutes.

She is not like the other girls who have inhabited my rooms, not the typical sour-eyed Northerner. The American with the raspberry-red hair who lived in room three: she deserved little. She went on her way three weeks ago, before I threw her out. I made a bon-fire of her bedsheets, a grey perspiring snake of hairs and semen. The flames jumped gleeful into the purple, night sky. All traces removed. All remains. Fire is the cleanest purge.

Charlotte needs no purging. She is different: she would not scramble with the rest of us around the chairs. Charlotte with a soft 'scia' sound. Carlotta, in Italian. Carlotta, diminutive of Carla, deserves safekeep-ing. Such a quiet girl. Strings of Scottish red hair, glossy, spiralling red—like the chestnuts I gathered as a child in the park. And grey-blue eyes, which avoid con-tact. When I first collected her, four months ago, from the airport, she stared out the car window for the entire journey. She never met my eyes in the rear-view mir-ror. She stared outwards and skywards, as though afraid of street level. Perhaps the Bologna sky did not look so different from the Scottish sky she had just left. All young girls need comfort. Even the wide, blue sky can serve. You see a familiar face there, perhaps, if you look. A watcher's tender face.

Five minutes more.

From the start, I knew Carlotta was different. It took only seven nights to be certain. Ribs of light glimmered every night through her shutters. You could tell a clock by her glimmering shutters. She studied; she put out the light; she fell asleep. She reminds me of myself. She defers her pleasures. She thinks there is a fairness to the world.

The other girls know better. They become themselves at night, return to Northern ways in the dark, think their doors, locked, and the shutters, pulled to, hide them. They allow themselves a smile, lie back in bed and listen for the rustling of male cicadas. The song pulses through their nerves. Night-time maracas. They sigh; the legs loosen; the too pale skin dampens. They bring in men—greasy-haired men who slope barefoot across my marbled floors. And then I pick up the phone and tell the fathers. Some fathers care and some do not. I usually give the girl a week's notice, in any case. It is stated clearly enough in the contract: no male visitors after ten o'clock. They are my tenants. My apartment. There is no point if they do not want my sanctuary. I will not lend my roof to pregnancy or rape or heartbreak. No more ghosts.

Carlotta always seemed safe until today.

I watched her from my window this morning. It is easier now that it is summer. She opens her shutters earlier and closes them later. The lemon blossom and the purple hydrangea float in the courtyard below. You think you could almost sail across to her window upon the clouds of loosening leaves and petals. Summer-time is my friend.

She got up at ten minutes past seven, early for a Saturday. She did not spend any time looking out, as she sometimes does. She squirmed into her denim jacket and tugged her small turquoise rucksack on her back. Her pale fingers grabbed a book from her desk. I saw her hand and I went over to polish the floors, a little earlier than usual. 'Gone out with her Italian boy-friend', one of the Italian girls, room two, smiled. She expected an arched eyebrow. I did not oblige. A land-lord must never react. Never show your sensitivities. Stay master, even if you dislike the role.

'A day trip to Florence,' the girl went on. She was sitting at the kitchen table, sipping an espresso. 'She was very excited, Signor Pellegrini. She wants to see the Uffizi and Ponte Vecchio. And David, of course.'

'David? Is that her boyfriend's name?'

A snigger of coffee splattered across her lips.

'David! You know? Michelangelo's David. The na-ked David.'

I turned towards the door and told her that they all needed to clean the kitchen more often. There are drools of week-old coffee on the hob, dribbles of to-mato on the floor, flakes of morning pastries scattered across the table. I told her I was sick of cleaning up af-ter them. A girls' apartment should not know such squalor.

She slurped her coffee.

I peeped into Carlotta's room while I was there. I cannot help myself sometimes. The window should be enough. There is a fragrance to her room that I cannot name—a fruit that I have never come across. Splashes of red and orange tease your eyes across her room, posters, embroidered cushions, drapes of spangled cloth. A mobile dangles by her window. Three lime-blue birds float. You open the door and the birds flutter into chimes. A pretty kind of alarm.

Two minutes.

Her room was not as tidy as before. A wine-stained copy of Dante's *Purgatory* lay splayed open on her pillow. Purgatory is the least comforting of the three. Neither the vengeance of Hell nor the tedium of Paradise. Purgatory is the world we already know, my teacher used to say. The discomfort we wear every day. The pavements and staircases we tread day in and day out. The dust on the underside of chair arms. The paper cups bleeding coffee beside half-empty bins. The cigarette chill of railway platforms. The stopped clock. It is hell in pencil draft. A first sketch after the event. 10.26. The moment you revisit for the rest of your life until absolution.

Charlotte is too young to understand. She is too young yet to have such memories. The fire that splintered the waiting-room windows. The dead girl that gazed in embarrassed surprise as you peeled your bloodied body off hers. The silence that fell across the city, street after street, room after room: a lazy power cut. The dead girl's eyes, grey-blue, that begged you not to leave.

'Il treno delle 22.33 proveniente da Firenze è in arrivo al binario uno.'

Carlotta is coming.

Soon, her perfume will blossom through the station. The unknown fruit. A winter fruit, like tangerines or clementines. A fruit to powder in warm cinnamon.

I stroll across to the newsstand and flick my chewing gum in the bin. The old woman bleeds plum-coloured lipstick as she hands me a copy of *L'Epoca*.

Passengers from Florence drift across the concourse as I turn my back and concentrate on the front cover. Berlusconi smirks up at me. A middle-aged man in a mole-brown suit trots past; a young mother slouches towards the exit, a toddler's flushed face nodding over her shoulder; a skinny young man twirls like a pop singer in front of a laughing girl. The man has the purple backpack strapped to his shoulders. The burgundy towel in his backpack is fresh from the laundry. No speckles of sand. It is tomorrow that he will go to the beach. He and his girlfriend will let their bodies sink together into the soft, demerara sand. No clock.

I swipe at the front cover of my magazine.

Another four or five people trail towards the exit. No spirals of red hair. No Christmas perfume.

I turn and look towards the platform. I don't care if she realises. I must know she is safe, even if she is with him and they linger beneath the arch in some kind of mumbling embrace.

The train heaves away from the platform. Windows blur one into the other. A paper cup rattles against the wall.

Carlotta has not come home. She is with him, out of my safekeeping.

The silence is here again. Everyone must hear it now, as it settles like white dust on the tracks and the benches, as it powders people's eyelids and hair and curled hands. Plastercast bodies, like Pompeii. The blood trickles across the girl's forehead again. Her blinded eyes stare. She asks me who I am. I open my mouth but I cannot find my name.

Elisabetta was her name. I saw her photograph in the newspaper the day after. Aged seventeen. Elisabetta. Isa, for short.

Her hand trembles at my shoulder. A ragged fingernail scratches through my cotton shirt. She cries God's name. She asks for his help.

I laugh. My shy horror is the last sound she hears.

I stumble towards the exit and inhale the iced air.

Charlotte is like all the others. She does not want my safekeeping. Her hand will not stay on my shoulder. I will never hear her say thank you.

I will phone her father tomorrow.

He will laugh, perhaps, in shy horror.

Claudia Boers

The Imperfect Roundness of Things

Even from a distance, seen as a small solitary figure with a backdrop of churning sea and cloud bearing down on her, Marianne was distinctive. She walked tall and remarkably upright for someone in her fifties, as if bending into and yielding to the blustering wind might be a cop out, or an admission of defeat. Even her skirt billowed and flapped and snapped about her ankles with rigorous abandon. Her hair was pinned up in one of those effortless styles Scandinavian women manage so well, a few white wisps streaming behind her like ghostweeds in a current. Occasionally, she stopped and hugged her long arms to her chest while staring out to sea, but mostly she paced the threshold of shore as if she had somewhere urgent to be.

The day was hesitating near the horizon. It couldn't come quickly enough for Marianne who'd foolishly hoped some lifting of spirits might come with the light, but the day was struggling too, only just managing to be flat and grey. She longed to be home, away from this soggy little island, to be reading her books or marking papers on the veranda while the sun shone and birds sang. Her visit had been a failure. She hadn't done what she'd come to do – she still hadn't told Freya. Things had conspired against her, but she'd been a coward too.

Freya was suddenly grown up, a woman of twenty-three. For the first time Marianne had realised how fragile their bond had become, how little sway she now held over her daughter's life. She bent down to pick up a perfectly rounded pebble from the sleek shore. She felt its weight in her hand, its solid, self-contained simplicity, and wished she believed in the absolving straightforwardness of fate. But fate, she knew, had only been invented to disguise the cruelty of life.

. . .

She checked her watch again. Perhaps, with the two-hour time difference, she'd catch Michael at his desk. They hadn't spoken since her departure nine days ago – it had been impossible to call him with Freya around. She'd only managed once, from a call box, after contriving to go out alone.

"Why don't I nip out and get a bottle of wine for dinner?" she'd suggested.

"I'll come with." Freya had wanted to spend every possible moment with her mother.

"It's okay, I'll be fine." Marianne had kept her voice light.

"No, I'll come. I can point out the gym on the way." There was a need to show her mother everything.

"No really, Freya, it's not necessary. I fancy a walk on my own." It had come out wrong.

"Okay." Freya wore the same expression Marianne

had seen the day she'd suggested Freya, then twenty-one, might want to fly the nest and find digs of her own. Marianne had meant it well – after all she'd been independent from the age of eighteen – even though, if she was honest, she had to admit there'd been an element of desire for her own freedom too. But it hadn't been just that, she'd wanted to protect Freya, her only child and someone who had a tendency towards adopting abandoned animals or lonely people at Christmas, from becoming a duty-bound companion to her widowed mother.

As she'd done the first time she'd seen that look, Marianne stood her ground. She'd needed to speak to Michael, alone. But it hadn't been worth it because in the end he hadn't even been there.

"Can I tell him who called?" His secretary had asked in a way that made Marianne wince.

"No. No message thanks."

She'd returned to the flat feeling guilty, cross with herself for feeling guilty, and empty-handed – she'd forgotten the wine. Freya had given her mother a funny look, but said nothing. Then surprisingly Jake had emerged from the bedroom where he'd been watching TV, and offered to go with an enthusiasm Marianne hadn't yet seen. He'd taken his wallet and newfangled phone, and been unusually long about it too, Marianne now recalled glumly.

She'd had her doubts even before meeting Jake, when she'd only had what Freya told her during their weekly phone calls to go on. Initially he'd been just a casually mentioned flatmate, from whom Freya was renting a room, but he'd quickly evolved into a cagily mentioned boyfriend. Not wanting to alienate her daughter, Marianne had accepted everything without comment. Freya never mentioned his age, and maybe because of this Marianne had guessed he was older. Her hunch proved right, but no amount of instinct could have prepared her for the character that greeted her at the airport – the blood-tinged basset eyes, the spiky black top and traffic-cone-orange combat trousers, the brutal metal-heeled boots, the potbelly, the self-conscious goatee, the complete lack of any sort of chin. It wasn't just his appearance that alarmed her – it was the challenging thrust of his jaw, the way he stood with his hands in his pockets. Next to him, Freya – tiny, fresh-faced and pretty – had beamed with equal measures of happiness and pleading. Marianne had forced a smile and taken the incongruously little hand that Jake thrust at her. She'd tried not to stare at the two points in his thinning grey hair where it seemed a pair of horns was trying to push their way through.

"You took a long way getting here." His voice was like a querulous old man's.

"Oh, I don't mind. I quite like having the time to myself, the longer the better as far as I'm concerned. More reading time," she laughed, but seeing she'd elicited a baboon's blank stare she added, "And who can complain when you're being waited on hand and foot? Though I tell you I could have done with a drink."

To fly any route other than the cheapest would have been out of character for Marianne. The extra flight time and a six-hour stopover in Dubai were simply a consequence of the best available deal. She came from a class of women who, though comfortable, never threw leftovers away and wore the same serviceable shoes until the soles wore out.

Jake strutted ahead as they left the terminal building. As they crossed into the short-term parking Freya pointed out his gleaming black BMW with such irrepressible pride that Marianne shivered in the cold, diesel-laden air.

. . .

Jake tapped the pack of Marlboro Lights on the bedside table until a cigarette nudged its way out. Why that particular one, not one of the others, wondered Freya? She often thought about random things such as this. Chance. Luck. Fate. Things just happened as they were meant to. Like her and Jake — he'd coming along right when she'd needed him, when her money had almost run out. He pulled the destined cigarette free with his teeth and lit it.

"Chill out, would you?" He sighed as two streams of stale smoke spewed from his nostrils. "I'll come out in a minute, I just need a bit of time to de-tune after work."

"Okay, but please don't be too long." She tried not to sound like a nag. "I'd like you to get to know each other a bit, that's all."

"For fuck's sake, Freya, we're going on a bloody four day road trip together. We'll get to know each other then."

"First impressions matter too," she murmured.

"What?" His eyes were back on the TV.

"Never mind. I'm going to make dinner."

She didn't want a scene, not this week. Yesterday as she'd watched her mother pushing her flimsy suitcase into the arrivals hall, as alert and bird-like as ever and thinner than Freya remembered, a sense of protectiveness had swept over her. She'd leapt in the air and waved without a care until Marianne had spotted her.

They'd embraced, keenly searching each other's faces for signs of change, even though Freya had only been gone six months. She saw the fine new lines, the even starker whiteness of Marianne's hair. For an instant she imagined she could reach out and, with the gentlest stroke, touch her mother's mortality.

. . .

There was a new quality about Freya, which Marianne couldn't put her finger on. She glowed with exertion and a sense of occasion, eager to prove her capability as she bustled around the tiny yellow kitchen, but every now and again Marianne felt an uneasiness creeping into the room like a silent third person. They'd had a busy day – Marianne making the most her time in London before they set off for Devon – and though she longed to put her feet up and read an English newspaper, she sensed it would dismay Freya. Her daughter needed human contact in a way Marianne, who preferred her books and a quiet academic life, never had. She was just like her father in that respect. From time to time it had worried Marianne that his early death had deprived Freya of a more gregarious childhood, but never quite enough for her to change her ways. However that evening, in the spirit of a convivial visit, she remained in the kitchen and they chatted about things such as Sally Holmes's baby, the oak tree being struck by lightning and the nasty new double story house next door. They were careful not to discuss Freya's lack of job, or her relationship with Jake. That would not be fair, felt Marianne, until she had first told Freya about her affair with Michael.

Over a supper of *carpaccio* on heart-shaped beds of

rocket, salt-crusted sea bass, and a fresh berry *Pavlova,* Marianne, who secretly would have been happy with a bowl of soup, tried to engage Jake in conversation. He was doggedly unforthcoming. It was only when she asked about his job in retail that he grew animated.

"I'll be a director before the year's out," he finished off. "One of the quickest promotions in the history of the company. Ever."

"Oh, that's excellent," said Marianne, looking at Jake's greying temples and wondering what he'd done before. "Congratulations. That's very good."

"I thought so too," said Jake and emitted a low wheezy sound, which Marianne recognised as a chuckle. "But I had to do it quickly, didn't I?" He took Freya's hand and gave her a proprietorial wink. "I've got to look after my woman."

Marianne fought hard not to raise her eyebrows as she turned to Freya, who avoided her mother's eye.

"But you're lucky Freya's an independent sort of woman, Jake." She spoke in careful, even tones. "She'll have a career of her own."

Marianne had planned to discuss this, as well as Freya's financial dependence on Jake, in private, but he'd forced her hand.

"How's the job search going, sweetheart?" She spoke with brightness she didn't feel.

"Oh, all right, I guess. I ring the agencies regularly but there doesn't seem to be much around at the moment."

"Really? There must be *something* available for a person with your qualifications?"

"It's hard, mum."

"I'm sure it is, Freya, but you've just got to start somewhere. Can't you temp in the mean time, just to get yourself out there and earn some money?" She tried to keep the irritation out of her voice.

"I'm trying." Freya sounded unconvinced.

"Well, ladies," intercepted Jake, using a term that riled Marianne as he mashed his cigarette into the ashtray, "Let's have some more wine. No point in worrying, is there?"

You puffed-up little idiot, thought Marianne, but she replied, "Good idea."

Later that night, as she prepared for bed she noted with a mixture of pride and misgiving, how Freya, first-time mistress of her own home, had put out fresh towels and left a small gift of bath oil next to the vase of Sweet Williams on the bedside table.

. . .

Freya was half awake. She was in bed. It was too dark to see anything. The steady breathing next to her was her mother. Though something was wrong. What? She'd done something wrong. Said something. She felt naked. As she swam up from the befuddled depths of sleep she became aware that she had no pyjamas on – she really was naked. She sat up quickly. She had to get dressed – she was too old to be naked in bed with her mother. Her mother would be disappointed in her. She paused, perched on the edge of the bed. This wasn't her mother's room. Where was she? With the slowness of a drunk waking after a big night, she realised she wasn't at home – she was in London. The sleeping form next to her was Jake. It didn't matter that she was naked. But still, she felt uneasy. She lay back down and pulled the duvet around her. For a long time, as she lay awake in the dark listening to Jake's heavy breathing, she felt an inexplicable and overwhelming sense of loss.

. . .

On the third day of their trip to Devon they sat parked in yet another empty parking lot overlooking another rainy beach. Jake smoked and drummed his fingers in time to the music. Freya hoped it wasn't too loud for her mother, who sipped coffee from a polystyrene cup in the backseat. It felt odd that her mother sat in the back, as if she were the child and Jake and Freya the parents, but she'd insisted, and Jake had readily agreed. Freya rubbed her naked eyelids (Jake didn't like make-up) as a baby does when it's tired. She was tired. Her weariness was laced with disappointment that things were not going better. They were struggling to fill their days driving between bed-and-breakfasts and finding places to eat. Where her mother tended towards exploring historical churches or walking on the windswept moors or beaches, Jake preferred the comfort of a pub. Caught in the middle, Freya found herself siding with Jake more often than not, simply because her mother was easier to manage. He'd been resentful even before they'd left – angry about wasting his annual leave – and Freya couldn't risk further exacerbation. The relentless cold and wet wasn't helping either.

She noticed an eyelash on her finger – she could blow it off and make a wish. She was always careful with her wishes, just in case they did come true. She didn't have to think long – the wish emerged as easily as a blush. She wound down the window and lined the lash up on the tip of her index finger. Then she bent her head so that all she could see behind it was the opaque grey sky – it was important that wishes were transported somewhere aesthetic, no point in blowing a wish into a gutter. She shut her eyes, pursed her lips and blew hard as she chanted inwardly, please let mum accept Jake, please don't let her be angry, please don't let her push me away. Technically it was more than one wish, but sometimes, when things were interlinked, you had no choice but to keep going until the circle was complete.

"What are you doing? Shut the window." Jake had finished his cigarette and was starting the engine.

"Making a wish." She hoped he'd think it sweet – that's what he said he'd fallen for the first time he'd met her, when she'd viewed his flat. He'd told her so three weeks later, after giving her a single, long-stemmed rose every day since their first meeting. He'd said she'd been the sweetest, prettiest thing he'd ever seen. All he did now was shake his head and shrug.

. . .

It had been the longest week, thought Marianne grimly as she headed back along the beach towards the call box she'd spotted on the edge of the town. This was the last place on their Devon tour. They'd arrived the previous night, too late for the tourist office, and had ended up driving around in search of somewhere to stay. After several fruitless enquiries, Marianne and Freya had been offered a single family room in a tired-looking bed-and-breakfast. They'd both hesitated (Jake had been waiting in the car) but had agreed to take it.

When Freya had told Jake with a nervous giggle that they were all to share a room, he'd slammed the car into reverse and backed into their landlady's crazy paved driveway without a further word. Freya had given her mother a helpless look and then rushed off to help him unload the car. Marianne had waited on the lawn, mentally calculating the thirty-nine hours until she left for home.

After perching on the edge of their beds while Jake made several urgent calls, they'd walked to the nearest pub in a fine drizzle and uncomfortable silence. When they'd passed the call box Marianne had suddenly longed to be within its hermetic glass walls, cradling the receiver to her ear, and pouring her heart out to Freya's father. Who else would have understood as well as Theo? Who else, but Theo, would have known what to say? But you couldn't call up the dead, and perhaps it was for the best because no conversation with Theo would have been complete without mention of Michael. And Marianne was certain that for all his encouragement that she find someone new after he was gone, her husband had not meant for her to take up with Michael, who had not only been his best friend and was Freya's godfather, but was also a married man.

If Theo were alive, she'd thought as they'd crossed the muddy car park, he would despise her for having an affair. He'd always been completely black and white about things like that. Like her, at one time. It had been that which had drawn them to each other in the first place. They'd met as students at a political rally when Marianne, feisty, and struck by a heady sense of affinity, had felt compelled to introduce herself to the long-haired protestor who had shouted louder and thrown more stones than anybody else. Even near the end, when his world was turning gradually grey, Theo had stayed unequivocally true. She imagined his voice now, earnest and low, warning her of the risks she was taking, of all that she stood to lose – Freya's respect, the friendship of Michael's wife, even Michael's friendship, her own integrity. But despite everything, she couldn't end it. Michael had reminded her of the beauty of life. It was as simple as that.

. . .

They'd returned to the bed-and-breakfast after a desultory supper and turned in early. Marianne had been unable to sleep. It must have been about midnight when Jake's phone had beeped and she'd heard him slipping on his shoes and coat and sneaking out of the room. Freya hadn't moved. Marianne heard the glass door at the end of the passage clicking shut and then she tiptoed to the window. Jake was on the lawn – she could just make him out by the glow of his phone and cigarette – walking in tight little circles.

Marianne climbed back into bed. "Freya," she whispered, "Are you awake?"

"Yes." She sounded hesitant.

"Who's Jake on the phone to?"

Marianne heard the bedclothes rustling as Freya sat up. She flicked on the sidelight and the room was suddenly awash with the sort of yellow glow you might find inside a cocoon. Marianne sat up too.

Freya's eyes looked wide in her tiny face, but she held her mother's gaze. She opened her mouth, but it was a few seconds before any sound came out, as if she were on a satellite delay. When it did her voice was soft.

"It's his wife."

"His wife?" Marianne's voice sounded too loud. "His *wife*?"

"They're getting separated," said Freya, as if this explained everything.

"But for how long? Is it because of – " Marianne paused. "Because of you?"

"Jake says they were having problems before we met, they would have got separated anyway." Freya had the same pleading look in her eyes that Marianne had seen at the airport.

"Oh, Freya." Marianne listened to the steady ticking of her watch. Then something struck her, "But I thought he was living in the flat when you moved in?"

"No. He was going to rent out the second bedroom to someone else – it was an investment property – but then we met and, well, one thing led to another." She looked like a small girl tucked up in bed with a temperature. They heard the door at the end of the passage open and click shut, then Jake's footsteps coming quietly towards the room.

"Is he definitely leaving her?" She felt ashamed asking such a loaded question.

"Let's talk about it in the morning," Freya whispered, as if Marianne were the child. She flicked off the light just before the door opened. Jake crept back into bed.

. . .

Marianne didn't sleep. She wanted to beat her fist against the wall and howl into the darkness for the shame and irony and sadness of it all. It was beyond her control to stop Freya from binding herself into a mess, like one of those tribal dolls made from tightly criss-crossed reeds that could cut a careless finger open. Freya would have to learn in her own time, just as Marianne had. She'd been seventeen when her widowed father had capitulated and let his only daughter throw away a hard-earned university scholarship to go and work on a cruise ship. She'd been back within three months only to find her father living with a flame she'd known nothing about, and her bedroom turned into a sewing room. She'd had to find her own lodgings and work in the china and glass department of a local store until the end of the year when she could start the course she'd originally intended to take, only this time paying for it with a loan. She sat up in bed, casting the memories from her mind. It was five o'clock. She rose and got dressed in the dark. Then she crept down the same passage and out of the same door that Jake had used earlier, and strode out into the wind.

. . .

The narrow band of morning, like a thin strip of greased paper above the horizon, looked incredibly far away. Marianne's footsteps slowed, her fierce breaths growing louder as she stood still. The call to Michael could wait. She moved closer to the water, only vaguely aware of her feet sinking gently into the yielding mud. A spent wave spilled over the shoreline and over her socks and shoes, but she barely noticed. She felt the weight of the perfectly rounded pebble in her hand. She stroked its smooth, unspoiled surface with her thumb and then closed her fist around it tightly. From a distance she looked like some great flapping seabird as she took back her arm and hurled the stone, as far as she possibly could, into the sea.

. . .

Years later, when Freya looked back on that unhappy

period in her life, she wondered why Marianne had never said anything against Jake. She liked to believe that all it would have taken was some little word, some sign of discouragement, to have nudged her on a different course. A course away from three long and destructive years. But she was her mother's daughter after all, and as such, she never asked.

It had eventually been her godfather, Michael, who'd encouraged Freya to pause and check her bearings. He'd been visiting England at a time when things with her and Jake had been particularly difficult, and had become instrumental in helping Freya find an administrative post at a university outside London. He and his wife, Jane, had extended their stay in order to lend Freya a hand with packing and finding somewhere new to live. The job and the move had only been a start, but it had been all that Freya had needed in order to change course and point her life in a different direction.

Jenny Barden

Propitiation

'I am rich Potosí, treasure of the world, king of the mountains, envy of kings...' (From the coat of arms granted in 1547 to the Imperial City of Potosí, in the Viceroyalty of Perú, by the Holy Roman Emperor Charles V, King of Spain)

Diego was twelve ladders down, more than six hundred feet, and he could not turn round because the tunnel was too tight. Only by wriggling could he work himself along, like a grub inside wood. The darkness was absolute, hot and stale, heavy with dust. He tried not to think of the mountain above him, squeezing his back. There was not even a glow to suggest anyone was near, only rumbling thuds and the sporadic trickle of falling stones, impossible to place. He still held the candle, as if by the force of his grip it might spontaneously re-ignite. He must have jerked it against the rock when his sleeve was snagged, snuffed the flame out. He tucked the stump inside his habit, between his hair-shirt and his skin; he could do that, just, with a shaking hand, feel the heave of his breathing and the damp of his sweat. Candles were too precious to waste. He had seen men fight over one that was dropped. He thought of God's grace. God was with him. God was light.

'*Is not light greater than darkness? Where light comes into darkness, the darkness is diminished, it cannot prevail. The life of Christ is the light of men...*'

He would not show weakness and cry for help.

Diego pictured the morning. When he had been seasick on the voyage from Seville to the Indies he had often looked at the horizon; he had found that settling, though the emptiness had awed him. Now he was ill because he could not find space. The faster he squirmed, the more he was hurt, skinning his elbows, bumping his head. He should have accepted the pads for his knees. He had no fat on his bones to soften the knocks. Even tucked up, his robes caught and dragged. There was no clear way forward, nothing level, nothing straight. The passage was a mass of entrail twists. His sight was gone, he could only feel: the gritty bulges of abrasive rock, gaps opening that ended blocked. He thought of the light he had last seen outside. He would conquer the dread that he was suffocating slowly, that the air was too thin for his straining lungs, that he was buried in the mountain and might never get out. God would lead him with an image of light.

'*Believe and be guided. Believe and never hunger. Believe and never thirst...*' This was the teaching of blessed St. Dominic. And Diego had taken that teaching to the *mingas*: the men who were hired to cut the face of the rock. He had preached it to the *mitayos*: the indigenous who paid tribute by serving their turn, perhaps a year under *mita*, made to work like mules because all the black slaves died. With the credulity of innocents they had offered their trust. In return he had given them the comfort of

God, along with candles and corn, weak *chicha* and coca as he had been advised. Their expressions had been his thanks. Coca was the means by which a *mitayo* endured, his cravings suppressed for food and sleep, coca that once only pagan priests had used, those who had worshipped Pachamama as goddess of the earth. But now every miner was encouraged to use the leaf, to free his spirit, and leave his body to work.

So much was wrong.

After five days below most were wasted like wraiths, but only the *mineros* in charge had any knowledge of time. The day was Saturday. Work would not stop. For some the labour had only just begun. In the gloom before sunrise he had seen lines of workers outside, huddled over against wind and cold. June was when the *tomohavis* blew, bringing sharp frosts and stinging sand. The men had crept like lice over skin, keeping to the mountain's folds, filing down into the mines: holes filmed with ice, grey and glistening like bloodless throats.

Before he had entered, he had wanted to protest, but he had held his tongue. Raw objection would achieve as much as kicking the rock in an effort to escape. The system was like the mountain; he had to move carefully to gain ground inside, guardedly and slow. Think of the light.

Only the top of the peak had been solid with colour, and that was radiant with a fiery glow, as though its point had wounded the sky. The light had been clear, rising above the sparkling chains of furnace fires: the glittering *guayras* that lined the ridges in spiny rows, wide-topped cones each taller than a man, pierced and lidded, used for smelting the Indian way, over dried moss, or llama dung, or the *ichu* grass which was all that grew on the rocky slopes and was always brown. Clear light above smoking shadows. Diego thought of it and gasped.

He was sapped by the heat. Summers were hot in Spain, and up in the sierra the winters could be harsh, but he had never known the proximity of such extremes; they killed any African. Even the natives could freeze to death in the open, and sweat to collapse underground. One of the labourers had been stopped and stripped where the last of the light found a way inside.

Bend, dog. Let's see what you've hidden. A silver turd for your whore...

Diego shuddered. The memory revived his shock. He could not understand the cruelty of such abuse: to strip a man in frosted air who had just emerged from the oven below. The *mitayo* had been weakened from days of carrying rock. He had fallen quaking in a foetal curl. And the gate-keeper had laughed when he realized he was being watched, as if suffering was a game with pleasures that could be shared; Diego had put him right on that.

'Christ loves Indian and Spaniard alike, the Indian no less, The Spaniard no more. If you are poor, you are blessed, for the King-dom of Heaven shall be yours...'

What else could he promise? No more than comfort after death, as sure to be the innocents' as that light shone outside. None should doubt, as Moroti had seemed to, that in the eyes of God all men were equal. Moroti was a leader, but a leader who was learning. Behind his questioning was a child-like ignorance.

'Can your God see us when we are swallowed by the mountain?'

Answering had been simple.

'There is no place that God cannot be. He sees to the bottom of every man's heart.'

God could see in eternal night.

Diego was climbing in a crevice he could hardly squeeze through. Dust fell on his scalp and tonsured hair; it clogged his eyes and mouth. It was blocking his nose. But he would not panic. He tried not to pant. The only certainty in life was the certainty of death, and he had no fear of what lay beyond, though he had expected to spend much longer on the earth. The journey might be dark, but at its end lay his goal.

There would be light.

There was. Diego had been scrabbling upward, but he realized, looking down, that there was colour: a flickering orange. The light appeared as if from along a drain that connected with a sump deep below him. Writhing, he slithered back. The gleam became brighter. He heard Morotí's echoing voice.

"Fray Diego, Venerable Father, my brother…"

Diego dropped with a splash.

Morotí's grip was firm. If his own hand was shaking, Diego hoped that would not show. Morotí gave no sign of sensing that anything serious might have gone amiss, though his apology was immediate.

"Forgive me, Father, but the *apires* – the carriers, they block the way. I send them back. Did you have no light?"

His dark brows rose and knitted to form an apex of concern, and this was one factor that made him agreeable, Diego thought; unlike most indigenous, Morotí's face could be read. There was a Castilian expressiveness in the way he moved mouth and eyes. Full lipped and strong-boned, with a long chin and sloping forehead, he had the open, proud cast that Diego associated with nobility, though of course, whatever the man's lineage, and that was obscure, his circumstances suggested he enjoyed no special privilege.

"The flame went out somehow." Diego smiled quickly to convey that he thought little of it.

Water cooled his sandaled feet. A slight draught from an adit wafted sluggishly around his head. He was almost able to stand beside Morotí, though the man was tall for an Indian and forced to stoop. Diego breathed more easily. He supposed that instinct must have driven him upward, and taken him away from the main passage down, obvious now he looked at it. To the extent that he had ever felt a twinge of foolishness in recent years, he felt it then. Relief washed over him. If there had been a moment of weakness, it was uncharacteristic, irrational, and of no account. The company of his guide put him instantly at ease. He was touched by the way Morotí handed over his candle and prepared to lead without a light of his own. Diego lit the stub he had kept, and returned the gift with a blessing of thanks.

He followed Morotí's naked back, finely marked with vertical stripes: five lines evenly spaced that emphasized the length of his well-muscled torso, from wide shoulders to narrow waist; they were probably invested with some cryptic meaning. Each upper arm was also tattooed, ringed by a band, as was each thigh. Beyond a cloth round his loins, Morotí had discarded his clothes. Diego bumped against the tunnel walls, longing to straighten. The passage tightened until they had to crawl. They could not have much further to go, he reasoned; they were surely close to the bottom of the mine.

They were not.

Where the tunnel widened, men crouched. Diego shuffled past them to join Morotí on a ledge. He looked down. By his feet was a ladder, double-width, fashioned, like the others he had used, from twisted hide with rungs that were slack and far apart. It trailed into gloom, but its trembling suggested a continuation beyond, where men were climbing or descending in an abyss. Diego teetered and shrank back. There was scant space to stand until the *apires* had left. He watched them crawling with their loads tied to an ankle, each sack a man's girth, and over half a man's weight filled with ore and rock. In the cavern where he had preached he had tried hauling such a burden, and if he had been so encumbered he knew he could not have climbed back up. Without anything to carry he could barely face going deeper. But he would, if he had to. Already Morotí was crouching over the ladder leading down.

The left side was for descent, that was the left facing the ladder, and the rungs were spaced just near enough for stepping in paces from one to the next. Holding the candle was difficult while clutching with both hands, but it was possible, as he had seen Moroti do, to build up a swaying rhythm, using one hand only to grip the ladder, but mostly with the hand relaxed, merely sliding around the corded leather, while bouncing rapidly from foot to foot, dropping steadily in a backward stride. The problem was that the ladder was shaking. Diego felt the trickle of a fresh rush of sweat.

He breathed as evenly as he could. He waited for Morotí to go down further, and took a few plunging steps. His legs were stiff with incipient cramp.

The trick was to move the hands first, to resist the temptation to place both feet together. He knew this, but he also knew that the ladders could break when the thongs were well worn. There was no visible limit to the depth of the shaft. The ladder bounced violently and he tightened his grip. This had happened before. A column of *apires* would come up and file past, bent under the weight of the sacks on their backs. There was a glow beneath him, and the sound of shouting was ringing round the pit. He looked for Morotí, but could not see him below. He waited, clinging on.

The accents were not Castilian, but he understood a few words.

"Marchad!..." "Keep going... Move!..."

The *apires* were closing. He could hear their hoarse breathing and the creak of dry leather. A head became distinct below the flare of a candle; behind it was confusion. The shouting continued amidst whipping cracks. A man cried out, perhaps struck. Diego tensed.

Suddenly a scream broke out that went on and on, but diminished rapidly as if plunging over a cliff, and with the scream were bouncing thuds, also receding, noises that ended in a distant crump. Nothing followed. The shouting had finished. The *apires* were still. Diego scrambled down.

*

As he passed the light, he believed he heard Morotí, but not in any language he could comprehend. What was he shouting? The *apires* remained frozen, each hanging from one arm, eyes black and staring. Diego climbed down past them. Beneath an overhang, near the ladder's end, Diego found Moroti standing on a shelf. Moroti's hands were round a *minero's* throat. The *minero* was rigid, face upturned, mouth open, balance gone; his head was forced back and over the drop. Only the man's hold on the ladder kept him from falling into oblivion. And the ladder was swinging, pulled away from the rock, its anchor-pins loose.

"Moroti!"

Diego called and scrabbled closer. He came almost to the level of the *minero's* clawed hands.

"Moroti," he made his voice calm. "The time for this man's judgement is not yet come. Let him go!"

Moroti looked up, and Diego saw a savage: black hair streaming below a circlet of leather, teeth snarling, eyes wild, cheeks scarred as if by animal wounds. But in the moment of recognition that semblance was gone, and perhaps perception settled after the distortion of shock. He saw Moroti more clearly as the man he had first met: a leader, oppressed, but whose sensibility was transparent, his handsome face angled in sorrow and distress, a dark-skinned reflection of a familiar image from carvings and *pasos*, paintings and altar screens, but human, not sacred. When Moroti moved, he pulled the *minero* back, turned his head, and dropped the man on the rock-shelf in the manner of something noxious.

Diego was left shaking. The blackness pulsed as he looked down into the void, toward the place where the *apire* would be lying, unthinkably crushed. This was the focus of his protean fears. The body had substance, somewhere below, and by following Moroti he was drawing nearer to that. But he had no choice.

Nothing solid remained. A puddle shone at the ladder's base, and the water was red, though whether from ore or blood, or some effect of incandescence, Diego could not tell. Possibly there were tissue smears on the walls of the shaft, but the rock's natural minerals were sometimes coloured just the same. The water was shallow, he realized, stepping into it as he had to.

"The man..."

"He will have been taken."

This was all the answer that Morotí gave; he moved on quickly, and Diego had no wish to linger. He imagined the existence of another passage by which the body could have been quietly removed. The tunnel onward was almost a man's height, but so hot and airless that Diego kept his head down. By this means, he knew, he was less likely to faint. He fixed his focus on Morotí's back, ignoring all suggestion in the surfaces he passed, magnified by shadows and the glitter of crystal. Sharp hammering shook out dust. He advanced through a haze along a passage that reverberated with shuddering blows, and widened like a cellar beneath a network of pillars. He was in a labyrinth of stone, one so unstable that sound set it quaking; he was sealed between layers, like a mite in a tomb, scurrying in the lacunae of dry, decaying bone.

Apprehension funnelled his senses away from the noise and crypt-like smell. He kept his eyes on Morotí, and then, when he saw them, on the men at the workface: the *barreteros* wielding mallets and bars, the *apires* hauling loads, the builders shoring up the roof, and the boys collecting rubble. Here was life and energy, vibrancy and heat – most were moving with a febrile excitement. The men gabbled when they noticed him. A few even smiled. Diego turned to Morotí.

"Do they not know what has happened?" He was puzzled.

"They know, but the mountain comforts them."

One of the *barreteros* took Morotí by the arm. Talking volubly, he steered Morotí to the face and stuffed some rags in a fist-sized hole. He set the rags alight. Diego watched, amazed: that they should want fire in such a hell, that they were not spent and not weeping. He gazed at the flames; then he saw, above them, the shining trickle of running silver – the treasure that lay at the mountain's heart.

Diego bent his head, but he was aware of the workers dropping to their knees, hands joined in prayer, and voices raised in strange tongues, while Morotí was whispering.

"You have brought us good fortune. We give thanks to the one God."

"Praise him," someone muttered.

Was it his role to question? Diego gestured for them all to rise. His wonderment was such that he gave voice in chant, bidding Morotí and the others to follow as they might.

"*Laudate Dominum…*"

The oil of joy would be sprinkled over mourning. Though their hearts were heavy, they would wear the garments of praise. Beauty would rise from ashes.

"*Gloria Patri, et Filio, et Spiritui Sancto…*"

The mystery of the ways of God was manifest. He had reached into the heart of suffering. Despite hardship and loss the innocents sang out, no matter the means by which it had come about; it was happening.

"*Kyrie eleison…*"

Diego led them in chant and he led them in prayer. He recited verses from Ecclesiastes and spoke, as he had always intended, of the vanity of riches.

"The sleep of a labouring man is sweet…"

He wanted them to know that industry and poverty could be blessings, and wealth a curse. They listened intently, and then he bade them continue with their work; it had never been his intention to interrupt them for long. He left Morotí with the *barreteros*, driving a bar into a seam, apparently at peace. Morotí was fortunate, Diego remembered, free from subjugation, not abused like a *mitayo*, or regarded with contempt like those who were hired; Morotí worked because he chose to. Though what choice did an Indian have who had been displaced and dispossessed? The question turned in Diego's mind as he was led away by one of the boys, a little *siquepich* or 'backside cleaner' as the word meant in Quechua: one of those assigned to keep the passages clear for the lines of labourers who filed to and fro.

Diego gulped for breath as he groped his way back. He was bruised and aching, hot and exhausted. His ears were ringing, just as when he had passed through the tunnel before, except that in the clanging and hammering he could imagine the sound of bells: a glorious *campanada*. Diego had almost forgotten the *apire* who had fallen, but they were returning by the same way, and he began to see details that had previously escaped him.

The path was mostly dry, but near the shaft at the end large puddles had collected, filmed with streaks like crimson threads. And on these pools detritus floated: strands of wool, and the smooth ellipses of coca leaves. That was strange, Diego thought. The leaves could have been spilt from a miner's pouch, since every man chewed them, but there were many, and their density was greatest near a fissure in the wall, one that widened above a knee-high ledge. The ledge could have been why he had not seen the opening before. Diego paused beside it, looking at the leaves overflowing from the entrance to a small cave. He raised the candle, ignoring a startled cry, and the splashing that suggested the boy was rushing back towards him. Diego stepped up and into the cleft.

He saw and struck.

Diego hit with his fists in the grip of frenzied rage. He wrenched a horn from the beast and smote the thing with that; he attacked the perversion that he saw cradling death over its knees: a travesty of the pieta. He was David beheading Goliath, Gideon in battle and Gabriel afire. His wrath was that of Moses before the idol of the golden calf. He lashed out in fury, blinding the crystal eyes, breaking open the blood-caked mouth, smashing the grotesque erect penis, battering and pounding, obliterating the aberration until there was no longer any trace of what he had found, and the defilement of the corruption could be cleansed from his mind.

When he lifted the body, he did so from dust.

Jill Widner

Mina and Fina and Lotte Wattimena

Sumatra Indonesia, 1963

Across the street from the wharves where the oil tankers are moored, a row of white-washed cottages faces a tree-lined sidewalk. Except for the shutters, which are painted a variety of chalky hues, they are indistinguishable. Six white cottages. Six tile roofs.

There is a room for each of them on either side of a long dark hallway. At the end of the hall, a swinging door opens onto the kitchen, the dapur, as the girl will learn to call it. At night the long fluorescent glass tubes attached to the ceiling crackle slightly and cast a pale greenish light onto the bare white cupboards and walls.

Behind the kitchen, a breezeway overgrown with bougainvillea connects the back of the guest house to the belakang, a row of rooms built on a concrete slab, where the houseboy lives with his mother. Mangoon answers the door and brings cold drinks on a tray when anyone, even the small white girl, presses a buzzer on the wall in the living room. Mina does the cooking. The children's parents refer to them as the servants, though

Mina has told the girl that, in Bahasa Indonesia, Mangoon is the jongos and she is the koki.

Each morning at dawn, Mangoon makes his rounds outside. He sets the sprinkler. He opens the shutters. Then he walks to the belakang, where he steps out of his rubber slippers and enters the back of the house through the kitchen door. The girl feels his presence, barefoot now, padding soundlessly down the hallway past the closed bedroom doors to the living room, where he tips open the glass-louvered windows to let in the air, which brings with it the yellow smell of the river.

The clank of the tea kettle against the burner in the kitchen tells the girl that Mina is awake. She gets dressed, unbolts the front door, and waits on the doorstep at the front of the house for Mina to bring her a ring of pineapple on a small white plate.

Mina uses a wide-toothed bamboo rake to scrape at the concrete footpath that the thick roots of the frangipani trees have warped and broken in places, but flowers fall to the ground faster than she can sweep them into a pile. When the girl tells Mina she's thirsty, the old woman leans the rake against the trunk of one of the trees and beckons the girl to follow her to the belakang.

They enter the kitchen through the back door, the only door Mina ever uses. After she washes her hands at the sink—in a stream of cold water, the girl notices, no soap, no tea towel; she wipes her palms across the front of her sarong instead—she begins to perform what looks to the girl like alchemy, like magic.

Mina opens the refrigerator and removes what the girl thinks at first is a jar of water. "Air gula," she says, letting a little drip into the lid, which she holds for the girl to taste.

It isn't water; it is a viscid sticky substance. She licks her finger. Sugar water.

Mina squeezes juice from yellow-skinned limes into a glass. Sometimes in the evening, her son Mangoon brings drinks to her parents on a tray that he calls gin jeruk. This must be plain lemonade. The girl searches her new vocabulary, puts together the words for water and lime. "Air jeruk?" she asks.

Mina nods.

The girl wants to tell her that she knows the difference between the sour jeruk, the yellow skinned limes Mina is pressing into the glass, and the dark green, loose-skinned tangerines stacked in a bowl on the counter. She points to the bowl of sweet jeruks to check: "Jeruk nipis?"

"Bukan."

The girl likes the word bukan. It doesn't quite mean no. But she is reasonably sure that Mina has said no. In Indonesian, there must be a family of no.

"Jeruk manis, itu," Mina tells her.

"Jeruk manis?"

"Itu dia," Mina says, and from the way she nods, the girl understands she has said something roughly in the range of, that's right.

The girl is sitting cross-legged in the grass, holding the glass of lemonade with both hands. If air means water, then what can jeruk mean, when sometimes it can be a kind of tangerine and sometimes a lime. Maybe manis means sweet and nipis means sour. Or maybe nipis means small. Maybe nipis means small and sour with a tight thin skin that is sometimes yellow and sometimes green. Maybe in Indonesian, a single word can mean all of those things.

Mina, whose body is old and not much bigger than the seven year old girl's, is squatting now on bare flat feet beside the frangipani tree. Her sarong has been washed so many times that the color is nearly gone from the fabric. But what fascinates the girl most of all, besides the way she is able to tie her long gray hair into a knot at the back of her head with the twist of her wrist, are the circles of flesh, large as coins, missing from the lobes of her ears. Mina breaks a stem from a frangipani leaf. Sticky milk oozes out. She places one of the flowers on the girl's shoulder, who watches, mesmerized, as Mina lifts her arm. Then, as if she has commanded it to do so, the flower cartwheels end over end to the girl's wrist, which Mina turns over at just the right moment for the flower to fall into the palm of her hand.

○8

Elizabeth is kneeling on the couch beneath the living room window, her face pressed to the louvers in such a way that the space between the shelves of glass is like the eyepiece of a microscope through which she can stare at the rain dripping from the eaves onto the front step.

Her brother walks into the room, eating a piece of toast smeared with peanut butter.

"What are you doing?"

"Nothing."

"Why do you always sit like that?"

"Like what?"

"Backwards. On top of your feet."

The girl looks down as though she hadn't noticed her knees pushed into the crack between the cushions.

"I always sit like this?"

"Mina wants you."

"Why?"

"How should I know," he says. "I don't speak Chinese."

"It isn't Chinese."

"Bahasa, then."

Her brother licks his thumb and wipes the crumbs from his face with the back of his hand. Then a streak of made-up sounds slides out of his sneering mouth. "*Bekin-bekin main-main tak-tak*. Why do they always have to say everything twice?"

"You're not even saying anything."

"I think your little Indo friend is waiting for you."

"Fina is here? Why didn't you tell me?"

"I did tell you. I said Mina wants you."

"She isn't Indonesian, she's Filipino."

"What's the diff?"

"Where is she?"

"On the belakang. In the kitchen. I don't know. Go look."

Elizabeth starts to take a step when her legs buckle at the knee. She meets her brother's eyes and she holds them, pretending that nothing has happened.

"Your foot went to sleep, didn't it." He pushes the screen door open and holds it for a moment, surveying the rain. He looks back at his sister, sitting on the floor now, stamping her bare foot against the tile. He shakes his head. "You should act more like a girl, Elizabeth. And you should try making friends with the Americans. You think you're going to want Fina for your friend when we move to the new camp?" The screen door slams. Through the louvers she hears him running, the rubber soles of his tennis shoes slapping the rain-soaked sidewalk.

Elizabeth stamps her foot a few times, limps down the hallway, and shoulders her way through the swinging door into the kitchen.

Mina is startled and reaches for her chest. "Kenapa, non?"

"Di mana Fina?"

Mina is wiping watermarks from a glass with a white tea towel. Five water glasses stand upside down in a row on a cloth beside the sink. Even in the fluorescent light, they gleam.

Mina ignores the girl's question, examines the glass she is holding before she sets it beside the others, looks to the screen door. "Hujan lebat," she says.

The girl listens to the rain striking the metal roof through the screen. "Di mana Fina?" she asks again. She hears her brother's impatience in her voice.

Mina points to the back door. "Tunggu di luar, non."

Fina is waiting for Elizabeth on the back step, sheltered from the rain by the roof of the breezeway behind the house. The rain is louder here, falling on all of the different surfaces, the concrete walkway, the mud in the garden, the bougainvillea branches that have climbed the posts and attached themselves to the tin roof.

Fina's back is turned. She seems not to have heard the kitchen door open and close. Her long black hair looks very shiny in the rain drenched light. Her bare elbows are resting on her bare knees, which she holds apart. Her fingers hang down from her wrists, and her bare feet are planted evenly on the concrete step. Over her head where the tangled thorny branches have gone wild, the purple-red bougainvillea flowers look more purple than red. Like Fina's hair, they gleam in the rain drenched light.

Fina does not say hello.

Maybe it is because they are looking in the same direction, but it feels to Elizabeth as though Fina has read her mind.

"There is a name for that color," Fina says. "Do you know what it is?"

Elizabeth shakes her head no.

"Magenta. Almost. It is a cross. Something between Magenta and Purple Madder."

"How do you know that?"

"They are paint names. My mother is a painter. She buys oil paints from a catalogue. They sent her a color chart so that she can know which ones to buy. I like to look at it. I like the smell of oil paints. Do you?"

"I don't know. I don't think I've ever smelled paint."

"You never had the chance to finger paint in school?"

Elizabeth has forgotten.

"I love to finger paint. I love how it feels. The way you have to wet the paper first and how slick and shiny it gets. I like reaching into the jar. I like to use a lot. I like to smear it."

"I never knew whether you were supposed to make a picture out of the paint or out of the streaks your fingers left on the paper."

"There aren't rules. It can be whatever you want."

"Why do you always wait outside?" Elizabeth asks.

"I was watching the rain. I like rain."

"What is hujan lebat?"

"Hujan lebat?"

"Mina said it when I asked where you were."

"Hujan lebat is when rain falls hard. Then stops

suddenly. It's almost ready to stop now."

Elizabeth sits down on the step beside Fina. "I like the rain too."

Fina turns to her. "I know someone who has a goat. Do you want to see it?"

Elizabeth looks at Fina. "A goat?"

03

Mrs. Watttimena's house is a clapboard cottage, rusty red, with faded yellow shutters. At the top of the steps, on a clean swept porch painted the same rusty red as the walls, two rattan chairs face a low wooden table. Along one wall, a row of concrete pots, brimming with knotted roots. Above the roots, tall slender stems bend with the small weight of orchids suspended from the tips like purple lanterns. Behind the plants two house lizards blink on the wall.

Elizabeth runs up the steps and presses her palms to the wall. "I love cicaks!"

"Have you ever looked at their feet close up?" Fina asks.

"I know. You can see through them."

"Sometimes?" Fina looks into Elizabeth's eyes. "Sometimes you can see the heart beating. Sometimes you can see the blood moving."

"In the throat, ya? There is a little bump in the throat that moves. Like a swallow."

"The pulse."

"Ya, the pulse," Elizabeth says.

A tall, large-boned woman unlatches the screen door and pushes it open.

"Fina? Selamat siang, Fina."

Her knee-length skirt rides high on her waist.

Through the transparent fabric of her blouse, Elizabeth can see her ample low-slung breasts inside a lace brassiere. She wears her hair pulled back from her face, and, perhaps because it is twisted into a loose knot at the back of her head, her forehead appears exceptionally high. Her skin is a soft, pale brown; her eyes, heavy-lidded and dark, restful, patient, kind.

Fina reaches for Elizabeth's hand. "Selamat siang, bu. Ini, teman saya dari Amerika."

"What did you say?" Elizabeth asks.

"I told her you are my friend from America. Mrs. Wattimena is the librarian at the American School," Fina explains. "She'll be your librarian when your school begins."

Elizabeth looks from the woman's face to Fina's.

"Siapa nama temanmu?"

"Elizabeth."

"What?"

"Mrs. Wattimena asked me your name."

"She doesn't speak English?"

"Do you like to read, Elizabeth?" Mrs. Wattimena asks.

"Kami datang untuk melihat kambing, bu," Fina interrupts. "We came to visit the goat."

"Oh, the goat."

Elizabeth nudges Fina's elbow. "Why do you keep saying boo, Fina?" she whispers.

"Boo? Oh, bu. Fina laughs. "Bu is short for ibu. Ibu bapak means mother father. You can call someone who is something like your mother or father ibu and bapak. At school you can call Mrs. Wattimena bu guru. Guru means teacher. Understand?"

Elizabeth sighs. It is too much information to absorb.

"You may call me Mrs. Wattimena, Elizabeth."

"Why do you have a goat?" Elizabeth asks.

"Our gardener gave it to us. I tried to refuse. But the children were so excited that we agreed to keep it."

"How old are your children?" Elizabeth asks.

"Fritz is nineteen. Charlotte is fifteen, and Nicolas is twelve."

"But that isn't what we call them," Fina explains. "Except for Fritz. Charlotte is Lotte. Nicolas is Nico or sometimes Coco. Fritz is Fritz. His name is short enough already."

"Why so many names?" Elizabeth asks.

"It's too long. So we just take the front or the back and use that. My friend Dian, I call Deh. My other friend Fritri, I call Fit." Fina studies Elizabeth's face. Scans her body from head to toe. "Your name is too long."

"What should it be?"

"Eliza?" Mrs. Wattimena offers.

"Still too long," Fina says.

"You don't have to decide today," Mrs. Wattimena says. "We can think about it." Mrs. Wattimena looks from one girl to the other. "Now I will show you the goat cart."

Fina's eyes widen. "You have a cart for the goat?"

"Coco hasn't told you? Come. I will show you."

Mrs. Wattimena leads the girls through an opening in the hibiscus hedge, past a small grove of lime trees. Fina ducks beneath the sheets, stretched tight and pinned to a clothesline. One of the sheets catches Elizabeth's face. Struck by the taut smell of sunlight on cloth, she presses it close and inhales deeply.

Elizabeth runs to catch up with Fina and Mrs. Wattimena, who are walking the length of the covered breezeway that faces the row of rooms where the servants live on the belakang. The walls facing the courtyard between the belakang and the main house are windowless. In place of a door, a long piece of cloth hangs from a bamboo rod. At the end of the breezeway, she hears the sound of flushing water, then a hook coming out of a latch. A barefoot, bare-shouldered woman in a sarong knotted below her arms, pushes open the door. The woman is young and is not afraid to meet Elizabeth's eyes. She says nothing, but holds the door partly open for Elizabeth to see, and Elizabeth looks. Just inside, a few inches above the wet concrete floor, stands an ivory colored block of cast iron with a rusty opening in the center, down which a trickle of water is circling. Behind it, a long pull-chain attached to a water tank. High on the opposite wall, a small ventilation cut-out is covered with a thick wire grate. In the corner, a concrete tub is filled to the mossy brim with water. Standing on the ledge, which to Elizabeth, is about shoulder-high, a wooden handle nailed to the side of a tin can and a large bar of yellow soap.

The woman says something in Indonesian that Elizabeth cannot understand and lets the door bang shut.

Mrs. Wattimena is speaking to the houseboy, pointing toward a shed. The man nods, glances at the girls, says a few words, nods some more.

The goat pen is a three-sided structure attached to the side of the house. In the corner next to the shed, a tin-roofed lean-to provides shelter from the sun and rain. Fina is peering through the chicken wire, trying to coax the goat to come closer. Elizabeth crosses the courtyard and kneels to the ground beside her. She turns to Fina and smiles widely. "It has a beard."

"Sini, Abdul. Mari sini," Fina calls quietly, patting her chest.

Elizabeth studies the side of Fina's face and mimics what she has said. "Sini, Abdul. Fina? Why did Mrs. Wattimena say he looks like an Arab?"

"Because he has a big nose," Fina says, still patting her chest. "Arab people sometimes have big noses." She slides her forefinger down the length of Elizabeth's nose. "Hidung besar," she says.

"Hidung means nose?"

Fina nods. "Look. He is coming."

Except for the white tip of its tail, the goat is black. It has a long, stringy, black beard, a handsome graying muzzle, and soft, nearly black eyes.

"I like his horns," Elizabeth says. She strokes what feels like the surface of a stone. "They're warm. I like the way the ridges feel." The goat's horns are short and broad and thick, and, the way they grow back rather than up, and out rather than into a curve, makes her think of a head emerging from water, of wet hair pushed back from a forehead.

"I like his legs," Fina says. "Kakinyamu, kuat sekali, Abdul," she says to the goat. "Look how long the hairs on his legs are. And how black and shiny and nicely shaped his hooves are. Like sturdy little boots. You are very handsome, Abdul. You are very strong."

The houseboy is pulling the cart by the yoke from the shed. It is a deep metal box with rivets along the seams. Inside, a wooden bench just wide enough for two small children to sit side by side, divides the cart into two compartments. The wheels are tall wooden circles, the discarded ends of old cable spools someone has salvaged from the maintenance garage in the refinery.

The houseboy ties a short rope around the neck of the goat and leads it out of the pen. He nudges the goat back between the bars of the yoke and wraps a thicker softer rope several times around his chest and belly, then secures it to the yoke. He ties another rope to the yoke in two places and it is with this that he leads the goat and cart away from the shed.

The houseboy is calling for his son to lead the goat so that he can push from behind. Fina is climbing onto the bench, and Elizabeth is ready to follow, when she notices a small girl watching from behind the curtain covering the door to one of the rooms on the belakang. Her mother, the woman who had scowled at Elizabeth for staring into the bathroom, is sitting on the sidewalk at the end of the breezeway.

Elizabeth looks from the girl to Fina. Fina shrugs. Elizabeth tries out the phrase she has learned, "Mari sini," she calls to the girl, waving her hand toward the cart. She looks to the girl's mother. "Boleh?"

The woman looks at her daughter. "Mau ikut?"

The little girl nods.

"Okaylah," the mother says. She takes the girl by the hand and lifts her into the cart. Fina wraps one arm around her and grips the side of the cart with her other hand.

The houseboy's son who is barefoot and holding a bamboo stick, leads the goat and cart to the front of the house, where he stops, and, shortening the rope, reaches over the yoke to hand Elizabeth the stick, instructing her with his hands to use it as a crop in case the goat needs to be prodded from behind.

The goat walks forward and the cart begins to move, the wheels wobbling unevenly as they roll down the road. The boy takes his job seriously, looking back to inspect the goat, the cart, the girls and his little sister sitting between them on the bench. Then he looks forward to check where he is walking. His father, dressed in a pair of canvas shoes and the same small black cap, but a looser, more wrinkled version of the uniform the houseboy at the guest house wears, pushes from behind to help the goat with its load, keeping his eyes on the wheels which are wobbling out of synch. The boy turns around, almost breaks into a smile, then catches himself, and pretends instead to be biting the inside of his cheek.

When they return, the boy lifts his little sister down from the bench and carries her back to the belakang while his father leads the goat into the pen and rolls the cart back to the shed. His mother has gone to the kitchen to prepare drinks and snacks for Mrs. Wattimena and the two girls.

In the living room, Mrs. Wattimena directs the girls to sit on the couch, and, soon the maid appears, carrying glasses of tea and small plates of food on a tray.

Fina looks at Mrs. Wattimena. "I don't think Elizabeth will eat Indonesian food."

"This one, Elizabeth," Mrs. Wattimena explains, ignoring Fina and pointing to a kind of cracker, "is called emping. Emping is made of a local nut called belinjo. This one is kerupuk. Kerupuk is something like your potato chip, but it is made of fish or shrimp."

Elizabeth takes a sip from the glass. The tea is bitter and the temperature of the still air in the room. She looks to the unmoving blades of the ceiling fan then bends to the floor and squeezes the Band-Aid around her toe, which she sees now is stained with blood.

"I like ting-ting the best," Fina says. "Ting-ting is a

kind of Indonesian candy made of peanuts and sugar."

"Sometimes it is made of peanuts and sugar," Mrs. Wattimena says. "This ting-ting is made of rice and sugar and sesame seeds."

Elizabeth feels queasy. Can concentrate only on the sheer curtains moving infinitesimally in the slight breeze drifting through the screen, curtains so threadbare, they are transparent. A pattern of white squares outlined with silk ribbon and, at the corner of each square, tiny beads of something shiny. Pearls, she thinks. No. Not pearls. The ribbon is silver, not white. They are rivets. Tiny squares of metal. No. Not metal. Thread. Two miniscule squares of metallic embroidery thread.

"Elizabeth?"

Mrs. Wattimena's voice sounds as though it is coming from another room.

"Takut, dia," Fina murmurs.

Mrs. Wattimena frowns. "What is there to be afraid of?" She lifts the plate from the table. "Try a piece, Elizabeth."

Elizabeth comes to, as though from a trance. She looks at the plate. She looks from Fina to Mrs. Wattimena. "I don't like rice."

"This is different," Fina tells her. "It's sweet. It's chewy. It doesn't taste like rice. It tastes like candy. Just try."

"I don't want to."

"If you won't try it, I'll think you have no courage."

"What happened to your toe, Elizabeth?" Mrs. Wattimena asks.

"I stubbed it."

"Perhaps we should wash it. Come. I will help you in the bathroom."

Elizabeth sees the rusty opening in the center of the

squat toilet in the room on the belakang. The moss-rimmed concrete tub. She smells the yellow soap. "I have to go home now."

Mrs. Wattimena presses her hands through her skirt to her knees to stand.

Fina stands. "Terima kasih, Bu." Fina nudges Elizabeth.

"Thank you for letting us go for a ride in your goat cart," Elizabeth stammers.

"Terima kasih kembali, Elizabeth. You are welcome. Come again any time you wish." Walking the girls through the kitchen to the back door, she changes the subject. "Elizabeth?"

"Yes?"

"Fina tells me your family goes to the Protestant service at the church. Is this true?"

"Sometimes."

"And you attend the Sunday school class at the American school?"

"Sometimes my brother and I go."

"I would like you to ask your mother if my children Nicolas and Charlotte might go with you next week."

Elizabeth stares into her face. "I don't know if we're going next week."

"You ask your mother."

As they are leaving, Elizabeth notices Mrs. Wattimena's maid, standing at the end of the breezeway facing the lime grove, her back turned to the sidewalk. She is holding a flat, circular-shaped basket in her hands, which she is lifting in a recurring motion.

Elizabeth watches, fascinated. Listens to the dry sound of something coarse lifting and falling. Sand. Gravel. She cannot tell. Whatever it is rises from the basket in a single piece, a gust of white that folds over on itself in mid-air before falling like a wave breaking back into the basket. The maid catches the cloud in the basket and lifts again.

"What is she doing?"

"Winnowing rice."

"Why?"

"To clean it. To take the husks away. To make the insects fly out."

Walking home they do not speak. Elizabeth is thinking of the Indonesian word for water and the way, when written, in English it spells air. How the rice was like that. Water and air at the same time.

"Fina?"

"Ya."

"Air means water. Right?"

"Ay-yer," Fina says, correcting Elizabeth's pronunciation.

"How do you say air? The air in the sky."

"Udara. Why?"

"I just wanted to know."

ᶜ঩

From the doorstep where she is waiting, Elizabeth is studying the sidewalk. Wet with rain only moments before, the concrete has turned to a glistening sheen. When she sees them turning the corner, what must be them, a girl of 15 and a boy of 12, Elizabeth bangs the door with the heel of her fist, then presses her face to the screen and calls out to her brother inside, "They're here."

He is arguing with their mother at the end of the hall. "She can walk by herself. She can walk with *them.* I'm not going to Sunday school."

Charlotte's skin is light like her mother's. Her hair, crinkly and buoyant, like braids let loose. Elizabeth scans her dress, not yellow, not white, but ivory; pin tucks running like a cummerbund, around her slender waist. She stares at the piping at the hem of the puffed sleeves that billow around her slender arms; at the rise and fall of her small breasts when she breathes. The skirt of the dress flutters where it grazes her knees. Elizabeth follows the lines of her legs, browner than her face, to white socks, folded at the ankle above patent leather shoes.

Charlotte takes Elizabeth's hand in both of hers and says good morning. Her voice is like a morning bird.

"I am Charlotte."

"I know."

Charlotte's eyes dart from Elizabeth to her brother and back to Elizabeth. "Where is your brother?"

Charlotte's hand, the feel of her skin reminds Elizabeth of something. She can't think what. *The wing of a moth. The dust on the wing of a moth.* "He's inside."

"This is my brother Nicolas."

Nicolas's face is light skinned too, but drawn back and worried, marked with spots of acne, some of which, Elizabeth has noticed, are festering and ready to burst.

Elizabeth's brother pushes through the door and lets it bang closed behind him.

Elizabeth looks from the long-sleeved white shirt Nicolas is wearing to her brother's madras sport shirt; from the ironed crease in Nicolas's shiny black dress pants to her brother's wheat jeans; from Nicolas's polished leather shoes to the curved blue line at the white rubber tip of her brother's Jack Purcells.

Nicolas extends his hand.

Elizabeth's brother behaves as though he doesn't know what to do with it. "Let's go."

The four of them walk up the sidewalk, past the bowling alley, past the refinery toward the new camp.

Charlotte attempts to break through the casing of the expression on Elizabeth's brother's face. "My mother said your name is Michael. Is that right?"

"It's Mick. I go by Mick."

"Mike?" she asks, perplexed.

"Not Mike. Mick."

"Oh."

Nicolas raises his eyebrows in the direction of her brother's shoes. "Nice shoes, Mick."

Her brother shrugs.

"Show them the soles, Mick." Elizabeth turns to Nicolas. "They're blue."

Mick ignores her. Reaches for his empty shirt pocket. Rests his thumb on his belt buckle. Then there in front of the Wattimena children, pulls a package of Marlboros from the front of his jeans and slides it inside his shirt pocket. He stares long at the oil tanker moored to the wharf across the street. "Ever been in the river?" he asks, untucking his shirt. It is the first thing he has said to Nicolas.

Nicolas shakes his head no.

"Know anyone who has?"

"No."

When they reach the soccer field, Elizabeth's brother cuts a diagonal path across the grass, which is wet. The three follow mutely behind until Charlotte turns to Elizabeth with a string of questions. "What do you do in your Sunday school class, Elizabeth?"

"I don't know. I guess they tell us stories."

"Do you sing?"

"Sometimes."

"Do you like to sing?"

"Not that much. Not Sunday school songs. I always yawn when I sing Sunday school songs. I don't know why."

Charlotte laughs. "I love to sing. Of all the hymns, if you had to choose, which is your favorite?"

Elizabeth gives Charlotte a sideward glance. "I don't know. I guess I like *In the Garden*."

Charlotte hums one note and then another until she finds the interval she is looking for. "*I come to the garden alone / . . . / and the voice I hear, falling on my ear. . .* That is a beautiful song."

"What do you do at your Sunday school when you are not singing?"

Elizabeth tries to remember. "Sometimes the teacher asks us questions. One time the teacher asked us to imagine what hell is like. No one could."

Charlotte's pause is grave. "I can imagine hell."

"Do you want to know what he did?"

"If you want to tell me."

"He asked for a volunteer. I like to volunteer, so I raised my hand. He told everyone to follow him out of the classroom and into the hallway. There is a closet in the hall. He opened the door and told me to go inside. I did. Everyone was watching. He told me to close my eyes and to keep them closed. He told me not to speak. I did. And then he closed the door. I heard the key turning in the latch. No one said anything."

"It doesn't sound like a very nice game." The look on Charlotte's face is somber.

"I didn't know how long I was supposed to wait."

Nicolas interrupts, his eyes very serious. "Who did this to you?"

"One of the teachers. I don't remember his name. The one who rides the Vespa. He isn't a real teacher. He only teaches Sunday School. Sometimes he takes us for rides. Sometimes he lets us steer. Sometimes he makes it sway. It's fun."

"What did you do?"

"After a little while, I told him I wanted to come out. He opened the door when I asked him to. Then he asked me to tell everyone what it was like."

"What did you say?"

"I said it was dark. He asked me how it felt to be inside. I said I felt alone. I wanted to say I felt hungry, but I said I felt afraid. I think that's what he wanted me to say. Sometimes I can guess what people want me to say. He turned to the class standing behind him and said, 'That is what hell is like.'"

"Elizabeth?" her brother says. "Are you sure all of that really happened? Because I think you might be making part of that up."

"It did happen."

Her brother shrugs, his attention gone. "I doubt it."

"Who is that?" Elizabeth asks, pointing across the field to three boys approaching on bicycles.

The boy in the lead steers effortlessly, his arms crossed over his chest. As he approaches the center of the field, he looks over his shoulder, and, seeing that the other two boys are struggling to keep up on their fat-tired Schwinns; are standing now on their pedals, pumping hard to make their way through the long wet grass, he reaches for the handlebars and circles back. At first it looks as if he is zigzagging to avoid the bare patches in the field that the rain has turned to puddles. He bends over the bar of his racing bike, then, leaning away from the frame, his rear end, jutted into the air, sends a spray of mud from his rear tire onto the arms and knees and into the faces of the two boys lagging behind. He looks over his shoulder and grins, and, though they are red-faced and sweating and splattered with mud, they smile back, their teeth bared like dogs.

When they reach the group, the boys bring their bikes to a halt, the forced smiles gone from their faces and look from Mick to his sister through their handlebars.

The boy on the racing bike leans forward, chest parallel to the bar, rear end cocked above the seat, and, gripping his handbrakes, balances for a moment, pedaling backwards, the lines of his long lean back, visible through his damp t-shirt. He drops to the seat and plants his bare feet on the ground. "Got the goods?"

Elizabeth's brother pats his shirt pocket.

"What are you waiting for? Pass them around."

"Later," Elizabeth's brother mutters, rolling his eyes in the direction of the two Indonesians, standing to the side in their Sunday school clothes, so quiet they are nearly invisible.

"Aren't you going to introduce us to your friends?" one of the red-faced boys says to Elizabeth's brother.

"They're my little sister's friends."

Elizabeth looks at her brother. "We have to go now, Mick."

"I know who she is," the boy on the racing bike says, nodding at Charlotte. "Your mother is Mrs. Wattimena. The librarian."

The boy with the freckles sneers. "You let your little sister have Indonesian friends? Better keep your eye on her or she'll turn out like the Yoder sisters. You ever seen them walking down the street with their Indonesian girlfriends, holding hands?" He lifts his chin at

Charlotte. "Why do you all do that? Does that mean you like each other?"

Charlotte doesn't answer. Her face remains serene.

"The guys do it too," the other boy says, nudging his brother. "Do you do that?" he asks, raising his eyebrows at Nicolas. "Hold hands with your friends?" He starts to laugh.

Nicolas's face has turned to ash. He says something only his sister can hear. Turns his back on the group and walks away. Charlotte calls after him, but he doesn't respond. She doesn't persist.

Elizabeth turns to her brother. "We're going to be late, Mick. Let's go."

"Let's not, and say we did. Okay?"

The boys laugh.

"We said we were going to take Charlotte and Nicolas to Sunday school."

"Maybe you did. I didn't. Let's get out of here," he says to his friends.

The two brothers push their bikes across the field, walking this time. The boy on the racing bike looks at Charlotte and pats the gold bar between his legs. "Want to go for a ride first?"

Charlotte turns away.

He turns to Elizabeth. "Do you?"

"We have to go."

Walking home in the afternoon heat, Charlotte begins to hum. "Shall I teach you something, Elizabeth?"

Elizabeth looks into her silky dark eyes. "Okay."

"Pinggang, Panas, Pantat, Pegel, Lemah, Leti, Lesu, Lemes, Laper lagi, Laper lagi."

"What?"

"It is a kind of nonsense talk. "It is sometimes nice

to talk nonsense when you are tired." She looks at Elizabeth. "Or when you are confused. Pinggang, Panas, Pantat, Pegel, Lemah, Leti, Lesu, Lemes, Laper lagi, Laper lagi. Do you recognize any of the words?"

"I know that panas means hot."

"Good! You don't recognize how to say you are hungry?"

Elizabeth shakes her head no.

"Are you hungry now?"

"Yes."

"Laper, saya. Say it."

"Laper, saya."

"Good! Your pronunciation is very good. There are four P-words: Pinggang, Panas, Pantat, Pegel, and eight L-words: Lemah, Leti, Lesu, Lemes, Laper lagi, Laper lagi." Charlotte pauses. "I'm not so sure you will understand if I translate one word at a time. It is more a feeling. A physical feeling in the lower body. The feeling you get when the muscles of your legs are stiff. And your skin feels hot. Like a fever." Her hands circle her waist. "Here." Then her palms slide over the skirt of her pale dress and down the backs of her buttocks. "And here. Pinggang, panas, pantat, pegel. Lemah makes a bridge. I don't know how to say it. When a word has more than one meaning at the same time. Do you know what I mean?"

Elizabeth shakes her head no.

"Lemah can mean a feeling of weakness in the body, or it can mean the kind of weakness you feel when you are falling asleep. But also?" Charlotte holds Elizabeth's eyes. They gaze into hers as though she can sense what Charlotte will say before she speaks. "Perhaps I should not say."

"I want you to."

"Lemah is also what we say when an argument is weak."

Elizabeth is silent.

"When an argument is unconvincing. I don't know how to say what I mean. When someone has a belief that is not accurate." She pauses. "For example, the misunderstanding your brothers' friends have about Indonesian people."

"My brother is different when he is with them. Even with me."

Charlotte looks at Elizabeth. "You love your brother?"

Elizabeth nods.

"I believe you." Charlotte shakes her hair away from her face, lifts it away from the back of her neck. "Shall I tell you more?"

Elizabeth nods.

"Do you know the sound of a fading radio? Or the way a flashlight behaves when the batteries are running low?"

Elizabeth smiles.

"Lemah can also mean that. Which makes the next bridge. To leti and lesu. Do you know the feeling you have when your brain is so tired, maybe from studying, that you can no longer hold your eyes open? Or the feeling you get before you faint." She looks at Elizabeth. "Have you ever fainted?"

"I don't think so."

It is a kind of thirst. "Like a flower that wants water. A kind of hunger." Charlotte can see that Elizabeth does not understand. "I think you will recognize the last part: Laper lagi. Laper lagi."

Elizabeth's eyes are shining. "I am hungry?"

"Almost. It means I am hungry again. I am hungry

for more."

Elizabeth smiles. "I don't really get it. But I like it."

When they reach the hibiscus hedge that borders the pasanggrahan, Charlotte pauses at a narrow path Elizabeth has not noticed before.

"I will leave you here. It is a shortcut." She looks into Elizabeth's face. "Would you like me to show you something?"

Elizabeth nods.

"Tidak laper? You are not hungry?"

Elizabeth smiles. "Not yet."

"Belum. Belum means not yet. Then come."

The path is a dirt track between the bowling alley and the hibiscus hedge. The stucco wall is splattered with mud where the groundwater has stained the foundation. The roof is constructed of deteriorated sheets of corrugated iron. The ridges are mossy, the furrows, puddled with rusty rainwater. Elizabeth hadn't known there were rooms behind the bowling alley. Through the windows she can see cardboard boxes stacked on a table, the tops folded over and tucked closed. Upended school desks and a few broken chairs are pushed against a wall. Rolls of maps, unfurled across a wooden table. Beneath the table, a bundle of broken down cardboard boxes. One of them is flattened. Lies in the middle of the floor like a mattress.

"It used to be part of the Dutch school."

"The Dutch school?"

"Before the Americans, it was the British. Before the British, it was the Dutch."

Elizabeth doesn't understand. "What was?"

Charlotte points over the low metal roof of the bowling alley to the high-pitched red tile roof of the building behind. "The nice white buildings with the red tile roofs? The ones in Kampung Baru closest to the river—Jalan Musi, Jalan Gajah, Jalan Macan—even your guest house. They were built by the Dutch."

"And this is where the Dutch children went to school?" Elizabeth asks.

Charlotte points to the end of the path. Her finger arches in a curve to the left. "The classrooms were in the nice white buildings. I think maybe this part behind the bowling alley was the belakang for the school. Maybe the night watchman lived in these rooms. Or the gardener. That was before. Now it is used for storage. Sometimes boys go inside to smoke cigarettes. Sometimes they make a fire in a can. Sometimes with a burnt stick, they write on the walls."

"American boys?"

"Indonesian boys. The American boys go inside other buildings in Kampung Baru. You know the alley behind the American school in Kampung Baru?"

Elizabeth shakes her head no.

"You will know." Charlotte says.

The end of the path borders a tall fence that leans with the weight of a climbing vine entangled in the wire. Through the fence three concrete diving blocks stand at the deep end of a swimming pool, brimming with murky green water. "That's the old pool," Elizabeth says. "I didn't know there was a short cut to the old pool."

"The old pool?"

Elizabeth hears her brother's voice in her head: *The tile is mossy. The water smells like the swamp. No one swims in the old pool.* She looks into Charlotte's eyes. She cannot think of anything to say.

When they come to the gravel road at the end of the path, Charlotte cuts across an open patio and crosses the lawn toward the white-washed building with the red tile roof. A sidewalk leads to an archway blocked by a tall wooden gate. Charlotte pulls a bamboo handle tied to a string. A latch lifts on the other side, the gate swings open, and, inside, bordered on three sides by the white stucco walls and tall windows of the abandoned classrooms of the Dutch school, a courtyard. In the corner, a rocky pool. A fish pond, Elizabeth sees, walking closer.

Charlotte tucks the skirt of her Sunday school dress between her knees and climbs onto one of the boulders. She slips her feet out of her shoes, unrolls her socks, and drops them onto the sidewalk. Elizabeth pulls off her shoes and socks and crouches beside Charlotte, watching the way she dips the tips of her fingers in and out of the pond. The water is full of life and movement. Blue winged damsel flies drift above it. A water skater skims over the surface.

Squatting at the edge of the pool, her toes pressed into the rock, Charlotte reaches toward a cluster of water lily pads floating just out of reach. "If you tap the surface of the water, the carp will kiss your fingers."

Elizabeth tries it. One of the fish rises to the surface and bumps against her fingertips. Her mouth falls open when she feels the firm, darting sensation.

"My mother told us that you are looking for another name."

"Not another name. Something shorter. I don't like anything that comes out of Elizabeth. I want something different. The way Mick is different from Michael."

"What about Liza. Or Liz. Or Za. I kind of like that. Za. Do you know Zsa Zsa Gabor, the Hungarian actress? She is very elegant."

"I don't want to be elegant." Elizabeth looks into Charlotte's eyes. "But I kind of like plain Za."

"Shall I call you Za, then?"

"Maybe. Okay. For today."

"You can call me Lotte."

Elizabeth's eyes widen. "Fina told me that. I forgot. She said sometimes you call Nicolas Nico."

"Sometimes we call him Coco. It depends on his mood."

Elizabeth smiles. "Just like my brother."

Charlotte is silent.

Elizabeth watches her feet, the soles gliding back and forth over the surface of the water.

"Za?"

"Ya?"

"Do you remember this morning when you told me what your favorite song was?"

Elizabeth stares at the ends of Charlotte's toes brushing the surface of the pond. Underwater a spotted fish swims past the water lily and lotus roots.

"Look where we are."

Elizabeth feels her heart beating. "I like water," she says.

"I do too."

"Do you hate us?"

"Hate you?"

"I mean my brother. His friends."

Charlotte looks at her. "The Americans?"

Elizabeth waits for Charlotte to say more.

"Jesus teaches us to turn the other cheek."

Elizabeth frowns, unsatisfied.

Charlotte points to the pink buds of the not yet open lotus flowers, standing upright, rolled tight, floating among the lily pads."

"The ancient Greeks believed that the fruit of the lotus flower had the power to expand the soul. There is a myth called *Ulysses*. A man takes a journey, and on his journey he meets a group of people called the lotus eaters. When they would eat the lotus, it looked as if they had fallen asleep. But really it was a trance. And while under the spell of the trance, they could have visions."

Elizabeth looks into Charlotte's eyes.

"A door in the mind would open, and they could understand things better. About themselves and other people. The Buddhists think of it in nearly the same way."

"What is Buddhist?"

"It is a religion. From China. The unfolding petals are said to be an example of the way the soul can expand if we would let it. And also? It is the only plant that can produce fruit and flower at the same time. "

"Have you ever eaten the lotus fruit?" Elizabeth asks.

Charlotte smiles. "I have only read about it."

"I think there is something to learn from this flower. I like the way the blossoms are delicate and open, while the stems and roots underwater are strong and indestructible."

Elizabeth dries her wet hand on her bare leg. Tucks it between her knees to listen.

"The plant grows from mud, but the flower is pure and beautiful and unstained. It can remind us to be outwardly gentle to others while inwardly tough with ourselves." Charlotte looks at Elizabeth. "Do you understand?"

Elizabeth looks through the surface of the water.

"Do you know what I like the best about the lotus

plant?"

Elizabeth shakes her head no.

"At its center, there is a seed case. And inside, there are thousands of seeds from which many more lotus can grow if given the chance."

Elizabeth holds Charlotte's eyes. "You're nice. You're like your mother."

Charlotte smiles. "Thank you, Elizabeth."

"What is her name?"

"My mother's name?"

Elizabeth nods.

"Frida. Frida Wattimena."

"Everything sounds like a song."

Ben Cheetham

The Hate Club

Upon returning to my hometown for the first time in six years, I wandered around for an hour or so reacquainting myself with the place. Some things were different, some were the same. New buildings had sprung up, old ones had been demolished. For the most part, though, it looked much the same as the dozens of other towns I'd spent time in during the intervening years since my last visit: the ring roads and one-way systems, the pedestrianised high street, the out of town shopping-centre, the light industrial estates with their call centres and warehouses. In other words, it was the kind of place where most of us live now.

McMurty's Department Store was about halfway along the high street, right where it'd always been. It looked the same as I remembered. The same illuminated white sign with gold trim over its entrance. The same heavy revolving doors with brass handles. For all I knew, the lingerie-clad mannequins in the windows were the same ones I'd drooled over as a teenager. I checked my reflection in the glass and grimaced. Two nights sleeping in my car had left me with dark bags under my eyes. "Nice," I murmured, pushing a hand through my hair and straightening my clothes.

Inside there was an atmosphere of calm, dignified, modest affluence. Young women wearing too much makeup stood behind the cosmetic counters. With quick glances, they took in my cheap clothing, cheap haircut and forgettable face, and dismissed me as someone of no interest either as a potential customer or anything else. I didn't mind. I'm used to slipping under the radar. That's how I like it. If people take an interest in you, they start asking questions. Where are you from? What do you do for a living? I live in dread of having to answer those kinds of questions.

I mooched around for a while, pretending to browse. Then I saw Robert McMurty. He was fatter, balder and his shoulders were more slumped than when I'd last seen him, but still I recognised him instantly. He walked with the same pompous strut he'd had as a teenager, surveying his little kingdom. The sight of him made my heart beat fast. I had to fight hard to stay calm as I approached him.

I smiled and held out my hand. "Hello, Robby."

He frowned, looking me up and down, obviously not recognising me. Then his eyes widened and, gripping my hand, he said, "Bloody hell, Tom, long time no see."

"It's been a while for sure. How you doing?"

"Good. Busy and stressed out, but good. How about you?"

"Not bad."

"You're looking well."

Still the same old Robby, I thought. Still a lying bastard. "Thanks."

"So, what are you doing back here after all this time?"

"To be honest, I'm not entirely sure. Can we talk somewhere private?"

Robby hesitated only slightly, but long enough to suggest some reluctance, before saying, "Sure. Follow me."

We caught the elevator to the top floor, to what'd been his dad's office. "The old man semi-retired a couple of years ago," he explained, settling into a chair behind his desk. "I'm pretty much running the business by myself nowadays."

"Sounds like a lot of responsibility."

Robby made a weary sound. "You're not kidding."

"You married?"

Again the hesitation, longer this time. "Yes."

"Kids?"

"My wife's six months pregnant with our first one, a boy. What about you?"

"I've never settled anywhere long enough to do the marriage-and-kids thing."

"Shame."

"Maybe. I wouldn't know."

A secretary brought in some tea. I thanked her and sat quietly sipping it, not looking at Robby. He cleared his throat. Here comes the question again, I thought. I could almost hear it buzzing around his brain. "Why have you come here, Tom?"

"I told you, I'm not sure. Do you see much of Stu?"

"No."

"How come?"

"I don't have much time for anything outside work these days." Robby swilled back his tea and stood.

"Well, it's been nice to see you again, Tom. I wish we could chat for longer, but I really do have a lot of work to be getting on with."

"Maybe you, me and Stu could meet up for a drink sometime, swap stories and reminisce about the good old days."

As I spoke, I fought against my natural inclination to leave quietly, to slink away like a man guilty of something. All I need is a minute, I thought, just one more minute to work up the courage to say what I've come here to say.

As if sensing this, Robby moved around the desk and ushered me towards the door. "Sure, that sounds good," he said unconvincingly.

He pushed the door open, almost pushed me through it. I felt a spasm of irritation at his touch. I turned to him, looked him in the eyes and asked, "Do you ever think about Martin Price?"

"No," he answered without hesitation.

"I do," I said. "I think about him a lot."

*

In some ways Martin Price was very different to the rest of us. He was more serious, more introspective. He didn't say much, but when he did speak, his words were slow and measured. Not the words of an average fourteen year old. In other ways, though, with his awkward, sweaty, acne-ridden body and bumfluff moustache, he was just the same.

The first time I met Martin, I didn't like him. His family had recently moved to the area. My maths teacher sat him by me.

"Where are you from?" I asked as the lesson

started.

"Shh," he said. "I'm trying to listen."

At breaktime I pointed out Martin to Robby and Stu, and told them what'd happened. "Sounds like a brown-noser," said Robby.

"Let's go talk to him," suggested Stu.

Martin was sat by himself reading a maths textbook. Robby snatched it off him. "Hey, geek, what you reading this for?"

Martin looked at him a long moment before he spoke. "I'm doing my homework."

Robby wrinkled his nose in disgust. "Nobody does homework at breaktime."

"I do. Can I have the book back?"

"Sure." Robby tore the book in two and tossed it back. We walked away, laughing.

The next maths lesson Martin pulled out the book held together by a mass of sellotape. When the teacher asked what had happened to it, he replied, "My dog chewed it." The teacher was angry. He threatened to phone Martin's parents and make them pay for a new book. But still Martin didn't tell him what had really happened.

I felt pretty bad then. I felt even worse when, during the lesson, seeing that I was struggling with my work, Martin turned to me and said, "No, you do it like this." He explained slowly and clearly where I was going wrong.

"Thanks," I said. "I've never been much good at this stuff."

After the lesson, Robby and Stu were still laughing and talking about Martin. Robby said, "Let's fuck with him some more."

"Leave him alone, he's alright," I said.

They looked at me, surprised. "I thought you couldn't stand him," said Stu.

"Yeah well, I've changed my mind."

I told them how Martin had kept his mouth shut about the book and how he'd helped me with my work. Robby grinned as if a new possibility had occurred to him. He took out his maths exercise-book, approached Martin and shoved it at him. "Do my homework," he said.

Martin looked the bigger boy up and down. His eyes were calm, impassive; they seemed to be judging Robby, seeing him for exactly what he was – a sadistic, spoilt brat who'd do whatever he could to make your life miserable if you got on the wrong side of him. In other words, someone it was better to make a friend of than an enemy. "Sure I could do it for you," he said, carefully weighing each word. "Or you could bring it over to my house tonight and we'll do it together."

"Why would I want to do that?"

"Because otherwise you won't be able to answer any questions in class and it'll be obvious someone else did your work for you."

Robby mulled this over, frowning. "Alright, I'll meet you outside the gates at home time."

The next day, when Stu and me arrived at school, Robby was stood with Martin. There was something protective about the way Robby was leant up against a wall close to Martin. They made an odd pairing – the overgrown bully and the scrawny geek. But nobody would've dared laugh at them.

"I reckon Martin's even cleverer than he looks," commented Stu.

From then on, Martin became a firm member of our little clique. He hung around with us during school hours. Outside school we showed him all our haunts: the off-licence where, even at that age, Robby could buy cigarettes and alcohol; the disused train carriage where we went to smoke and get drunk; Stu's dad's pub where we could play pool for free; the patch of woodland behind my house where we'd climb trees and light fires.

Most nights we ended up at Robby's house, a three-storey Victorian mansion like something off the cover of a glossy magazine. Robby had the attic room. His parents hardly ever came up there and we could play music as loud as we liked.

Sometimes, but not often, we went to Martin's house. His parents were strict Catholics and would stand for no nonsense. They kept a close eye on us. But that wasn't the only reason we rarely went to Martin's house.

Martin had a sister two years younger than him. Her name was Carrie and she suffered from severe epilepsy. She was a small girl, pasty pale with stringy blond hair. Her epilepsy made her irritable and the sound of her tantrums regularly filled the house. One time when I was there getting help with some homework, she came into Martin's bedroom and said, "I've got a funny noise in my head." Then she collapsed, teeth clenched, body taut and shaking. Martin cradled her head until the seizure passed. After making sure she hadn't swallowed her tongue, he put her into the recovery position.

At the time, it was the most frightening thing I'd ever seen. When I told Robby and Stu what had happened, Robby turned his finger in a corkscrew at his temple and said, "Loco."

Occasionally, on summer days, we caught a bus to the coast.

Three Rocks Bay was a popular beach fifteen miles out of town. The first time Martin went there with us it was a hot Saturday in early July and the long curve of sand was heaving with bodies on towels. We lay in the dunes, all of us stripped down to our trunks except Martin. He sat cross-legged in his jeans, a sunhat shading his pale face from the sun.

Robby ogled two bikini-clad girls who were a good few years older than us. They were busty and curvaceous. They had bleach-blonde hair and wore mascara and glistening pink lipstick. He nudged Martin. "What do you reckon to them?"

Martin barely gave them a glance. He shrugged. Robby turned to Stu and me. "Come on, let's go over there and talk to them."

Stu shook his head. "They're way out of our league."

"Piss off," retorted Robby. "They might be out of your league, but not mine. What about you, Tom, you coming with me or haven't you got the balls to do it either."

"They look like slags," I said.

Robby grinned. "I like slags."

"Well I don't."

Truth was, though, the sight of their fully developed bodies made me painfully aware of my still childish physique. I felt certain they'd take one look at me and burst into laughter.

As Robby got to his feet, two boys approached the girls. They were taller than any of us. They had chest hair and stubble. They made me want to put my t-shirt on.

"Fuck it," muttered Robby. "Let's go for a swim."

"I'd better stay here and look after our things," said

Martin.

"No chance," I said. Stu and me grabbed his arms and hauled him to his feet.

"Alright," he said, shaking us off. He undressed and stood hunched slightly, his spindly arms crossed over his chest. There were pustules of acne on his back and shoulders. The sight of him made me feel, for once, grateful for my own body.

Robby, Stu and me sprinted, whooping, down the beach and threw ourselves into the water. Martin followed more slowly. We swam out to one of the flat rocks that gave the beach its name. We dive-bombed off the rock, splashed and dunked each other. After a while, Martin got out of the water and sat on the rock, watching us. Suddenly, Robby grabbed my legs and flipped me upside down. He yanked my trunks off. I resurfaced, blinking and spluttering.

"Give them back," I yelled.

"Why, you worried what those girls might see?"

"More like he's worried what they won't see," said Stu.

Laughing, Robby twirled my trunks over his head and threw them to Stu. I lunged about vainly as they passed them back and forth. "Here, catch," Robby shouted to Martin.

Martin made no attempt to catch the trunks. They landed with a wet slap on the rock behind him. "Fetch them, will you," I said. When he didn't move, I added, "Go on then."

But still Martin didn't move. He was sat with his knees drawn up to his chin and his arms clasped around his ankles. His face was unusually flushed.

"Fetch them or you'll be next," threatened Robby.

Martin's face grew even redder. He was shivering as

though he was cold or in pain. After a moment's further hesitation, he stood and fetched the trunks. For once he moved quickly, but not quickly enough that I didn't see what he'd been trying to hide. I felt a surge of disgust. Martin tossed the trunks to me. I pulled them on and swam to shore.

Back in the dunes, I dried off and got dressed. Robby and Stu ran up to me, Martin following behind at his usual pace.

"What's wrong?" asked Robby as I rolled up my towel. "Can't you take a joke?"

I looked past him at Martin. His eyes flinched away from mine. I turned and started climbing up to the top of the dunes.

"Where are you going?" Stu called after me.

"Home," I replied.

*

I was still trembling when I came out of McMurty's Department Store. I hurried to my car and sat in it for half-an-hour or so, quietly pulling myself together. Then I got out and walked the short distance to Stu's dad's pub. I wasn't surprised to see Stu behind the bar counter. It'd always been his ambition to run the place one day.

From a distance Stu looked a little older, but otherwise the same. As I approached him, though, I noticed a moist sheen on his eyes and a network of ruptured veins in his nose and cheeks. His eyes narrowed. "Tom..."

I nodded. His face broke into a familiar, wide-eyed grin. "Jesus, Tom Reid, I haven't seen you since – well, since forever. How are you?"

"Not too bad. You know how it is."

Stu nodded and I caught a flicker of something in his eyes – some old memory stirred up by the sight of me perhaps. "When did you get back?"

"This morning. I've been walking around all day checking out the old haunts."

"You must be thirsty then. Can I get you a drink?"

"I'll have a pint of bitter, thanks."

"Put that away," said Stu as I took out my wallet.

He pulled two pints. We clinked glasses. "Cheers," we said, raising the glasses to our mouths.

"So what've you been doing with yourself all these years?" asked Stu.

As always, I winced inwardly at this question. "This and that. I travel around a lot and do a lot of temping. That way I can, you know, up and go pretty much whenever I feel like it."

"Sounds like fun."

I made no reply. Stu pulled himself another pint. "What about you? You married?" I asked.

"No, well, I was, but I'm divorced now. I've got a five year old girl, Megan. She's a great kid, really bright, absolutely nothing like her dad. Apart from that, since dad's stroke, I've spent most of my time running this place."

"Not much different from Robby with his shop then."

A frown of surprise passed over Stu's face. "You've seen Robby."

"I dropped in on him earlier. He said you two don't see much of each other anymore."

"That's a bit of an understatement. I haven't spoken to him in years. How is he?"

"Same as ever, only fatter and balder."

"Aren't we all."

"I invited him out for a drink. Told him I'd be in here tonight."

Stu snorted. "He won't come here. He wouldn't be seen dead in here these days. He's a respectable man now." He took a quick sip of his pint. Then, hesitantly, almost as if he didn't want to know the answer, he asked, "What did you two talk about?"

"Pretty much the same as what we're talking about. Do you remember Martin Price?"

Stu burst into a loud, seemingly careless laugh. But once again I caught that flicker of something in his eyes. "Martin Price, bloody hell, I haven't heard that name in a long time. He was a real oddball, wasn't he?"

"Yeah, well I've been thinking about him a lot lately."

I said lately, but I should have said for the last seventeen years. I should have said his memory follows me around like a shadow. Just follows and follows me, marking every moment of my existence, tainting everything I touch.

"Do you ever think about him?" I asked.

Stu sat silent a moment, not looking at me. Then he said, "I try not to." And he picked up his glass and took a long, long swallow.

*

During biology, when the teacher left the classroom for a moment, I leant in close to Robby and Stu and said, "Martin had a stiffy."

Stu sniggered. "No way."

"He did, I swear he did."

"He must've been thinking about those girls."

I shook my head. "He wasn't bothered about those girls, remember. He got a stiffy from watching us – from watching me."

Stu wrinkled his nose. "That's sick. Do you reckon he's gay, or something?"

"Course he fucking is," muttered Robby, his mouth twisting in disgust.

In a sing-song voice, Stu said, "Martin fancies Tom."

"Shut up," I snapped, shoving him. He made a kissy sound at me and resumed his taunting. I could feel myself blushing at the thought that the other kids might hear him. "You better shut your gob before I shut it for you."

"Yeah, shut the fuck up," said Robby. "This isn't funny."

"Alright, take it easy, I was only messing with him," said Stu.

Robby sat silent, face scrunched into something between a frown and a scowl. Stu and I exchanged glances. We'd seen him look like that before when he was really angry and not just acting. "That dirty little poof," he said, his voice low and full of malice. "We ought to teach him a lesson."

"What kind of lesson?" I asked.

"I don't know, but I'll think of something."

"Can't we just tell him we don't want to be mates with him anymore?" Stu suggested uneasily. He knew as well as I did that Robby had a tendency to take things too far.

"No way. We can't let him perv on us like that and get away with it." Robby looked sidelong at Stu, eyes narrowed. "Or maybe you like him perving on you."

Stu pulled a horrified face. "Piss off."

Robby turned to me. "What about you?"

"I'm with you," I said quickly. "He needs to know he can't mess around with us."

It didn't take Robby long to come up with a plan that appealed to his sense of justice. Early the following Saturday the four of us caught the bus to Three Rocks Bay again. It was a cloudy morning, with patches of blue on the horizon promising better weather. The beach was empty except for an occasional dog walker. We sat fully clothed, none of us talking much. Martin seemed subdued. All week I'd avoided him, even skipping maths. Now I noticed him casting sheepish glances at me. Under the grey light of the overcast sky, he looked even more pale and fragile than usual.

The longer we sat there, the more I felt like warning him what was going to happen. As if sensing my growing doubt, Robby stood suddenly and said, "Right, we're going swimming."

"It's too cold," said Martin.

"Don't be such a wimp."

We stripped off and made our way to the water, Robby walking behind Martin this time, Stu and me on either side of him, like guards escorting a prisoner. Stu's arms were hugged across his chest. He looked like he wished he was somewhere else. Robby had an excited little grin on his face that made me want to punch him. All the time I kept thinking, you need to stop this right now before it's too late. But I didn't stop it. I waded into the water and swam to the rock.

Martin hauled himself up next to me, shivering. He blinked at me, eyes nervous. I smiled at him. I've never been able to smile at anyone since without feeling like a fraud. We lined up on the rock and dived in. Robby swam underwater to Martin, grabbed his waistband and yanked his trunks off.

"Hey, give them back," yelled Martin, snatching in the empty air as we passed his trunks back and forth. Only Robby was laughing.

Martin's voice was angry at first, but after five or so minutes a pleading note entered it. "Come on, guys, give them back, will you?"

Robby climbed onto the rock. "Come and get them."

Martin clung to the edge of the rock, staring uncertainly up at him.

"What are you waiting for?" taunted Robby, dangling the trunks just out of his reach. "Afraid you might get another stiffy?"

Even in the cold water, a flush spread up from Martin's throat. He looked at me, scared now. "Please give me my trunks back."

Again I found myself thinking, you need to stop this right now. But still I didn't stop it. I just flinched away from Martin's gaze.

"Forget it, you're not getting them back," sneered Robby. "And we're going to tell everyone you're a homo."

"I'm not," retorted Martin.

"Then why did you get a stiffy?"

"I don't know, it just happened."

"Bollocks. You're a queer, a poof, a fag, a dirty little arse bandit."

Martin made a grab for Robby's ankles. Robby shook him off easily. Martin began to cry. "Please don't tell my parents," he said, his little-boy voice thin and weak, pitiful to hear.

"They'll be the first to know."

Martin moaned.

Grinning, Robby turned to Stu and me. "Come on, let's go."

We obeyed quickly, both relieved, I think, to get away from Martin. We made our way back to the dunes and got dressed. Robby bundled up Martin's clothes under his arm and started to walk off.

"You can't do that," I said.

"Why not? Who's going to stop me?"

I snatched at Martin's clothes. "Let go, or else," I warned.

We strained against each other briefly, then Robby let go and I tumbled to the foot of the dune. Stu rushed to help me up.

"You're a right pair of little poofs n'all," Robby shouted at us.

"Go fuck yourself," I said.

Robby glared at me a moment, clenching and un-clenching his fists. Then he turned and stomped off. I breathed in relief.

"He's a psycho," said Stu.

I laid Martin's clothes out on his towel and we climbed the dune. At the top, I looked towards the distant figure bobbing in the water just beyond the rock. For some reason, I raised my hand and waved goodbye. Martin didn't wave back.

Later that day I got two phone calls. The first was from Robby, sounding strangely nervous. He'd just spoken to Martin's mum. Martin hadn't come home yet. She was starting to get worried. "I told her we left him at the beach," he said. "I said we didn't want to leave him, but he insisted he wanted to be alone. She'll be ringing you soon. You need to tell her the exact same thing. Have you got that?"

"Yes." I waited for the call, feeling sick to my stomach. It didn't come for an hour or so. I flinched as if I'd been slapped when the phone eventually rang. I let mum answer it. A few minutes later, she knocked on my door – she never usually knocked. My mouth filled up with spit like it does when you're about to puke, as she opened the door. Her eyes were pained, maddeningly sympathetic.

"Something terrible has happened," she said quietly, almost as though she didn't really want me to hear her words. "Your friend Martin has been found drowned at Three Rocks Bay."

Your friend Martin, she'd said. For a moment, I couldn't speak, couldn't move. Then I bent forward and vomited over my lap.

*

Early in the morning, I drove out to the house where my parents used to live on what used to be the edge of town. The trees are long gone now, chopped down and uprooted to make way for new housing estates. My parents are gone, too.

Seven years ago mum was diagnosed with breast cancer. Dad phoned me with the news at the beginning of February. Reluctantly, I returned home. A week later we learnt the cancer had spread to mum's brain and adrenal glands. A fortnight after that she fell into a coma from which she never awakened. The speed of it all left us stunned and bewildered. At the funeral, dad shuffled around like a sleepwalker, looking like he'd aged ten years in a month, and I thought, he'll be lucky to survive a year on his own.

I knew he needed me, his only child, but I couldn't bring myself to stay with him. During the short time I'd been in town, I'd only left the house to go to the hospital and funeral. And even at those times, when all I should've been thinking about was mum and dad, I was constantly on the edge of panic at the thought of bumping into anyone who might recognise me, of having to answer their questions.

A few days after the funeral, I told dad I had to leave. I made up some crap about being needed back at work, but in truth I felt like if I didn't get out of there right away I might never be able to face the outside world again.

"You will come and visit me, won't you?" said dad.

"Of course I will," I replied. That was the last time I ever saw him. Almost exactly a year later he died of a heart-attack.

I inherited the house. My childhood home. I went there once in the middle of the night, like a burglar. I sat in the lounge for hours, imagining myself living there with a wife and a child of my own. I crept away before it got light.

I managed to hold onto the house for more than a year, before spiralling debts forced me to sell it. The day I handed over the keys, I cried as hard as when I buried mum and dad.

There's a new family in the house now. I watched them for a while. Two young boys playing in the street. Their dad mowing the lawn. His wife hoovering and dusting in the lounge. A perfectly ordinary domestic scene. It made me tremble to look at it.

Afterwards, I drove to Three Rocks Bay.

It was the first time I'd been back there since *that* day. I walked through the dunes to the beach and sat with my head in my hands, staring at the spot where Martin's dad found him naked. Naked and dead.

I thought about all the questions the police had asked after Martin died. How had he seemed that day? Had he ever spoken about any family or relationship problems? Was he being bullied? Was there any reason to suspect he was likely to commit suicide? When they'd asked me that my stomach clenched up like a fist, and it was all I could do not to puke.

There'd been more questions, enough to last a whole lifetime. And a lifetime's worth of lies to accompany them.

I closed my eyes. Robby's voice made me flinch. "I thought I might find you here," he said, sitting down beside me. There were bags under his eyes, as if he too hadn't slept. "I need to talk to you about Martin."

"He killed himself because of us," I said matter-of-factly.

"You can't be sure of that. It might've been an accident," said Robby, but there was no conviction in his voice anymore. Not like there'd been seventeen years ago when I wanted to tell the truth and he convinced me to keep my mouth shut.

"I've decided, I'm going to tell Martin's parents what really happened."

Robby's face scrunched up. He spoke through his teeth. "What good would that do after all this time?"

"I'm not sure. All I know is I can't live the way I've been living anymore. I'm so tired of lying to people."

"What about Martin's parents? Have you considered what it'll do to them finding out their son killed himself because he was gay?"

I laughed with icy contempt. "Surely you don't still believe that nonsense about Martin being gay? And even if he was, so what? That still didn't give us the right to do what we did."

"Don't you think I know that? Don't you think I know what we did was wrong? But we were just kids. Cruel, hateful, stupid kids."

"Cruel and hateful yes, but not stupid. We knew what we were doing."

I made to stand. Robby caught my wrist. "Please, Tom, I'm begging you, don't do this," he said. There was a genuine desperation in his voice that almost made me feel sorry for him. As if a sudden thought had struck him, he added, "I can give you money."

I yanked my wrist free. "I don't want your money."

"What do you want then?"

"I just want to come home," I said wearily. "And I can't do that unless I tell the truth."

"But you'll ruin everything."

"You'll survive, your kind always do."

"You don't understand. This isn't about me." Robby pulled out a photo of a heavily pregnant woman. Her smiling face and stringy blond hair seemed familiar, but I couldn't quite place them. "That's my wife, Carrie."

As realisation dawned, my stomach began to churn and my mouth filled up with spit. "Martin's little sister."

Robby nodded. "When she gets stressed, she has fits. And if she has a fit there's a good chance she'll lose the baby. She might even die herself. The last serious fit she had left her paralysed down her right side for nearly a year."

I turned away from him, swallowing my bitter saliva. "So you won't say anything," he said. I shook my head.

I returned to my car and started driving. That was weeks ago now, maybe months. I lose track of time. Some days I'm so tired I hardly know my own name.

I'm still driving, still heading from nowhere to nowhere. Staying for a day here, another day there, a week somewhere else. Scraping by on credit cards and whatever work I can get. Anonymous, transient. Nobody special. Nobody you'd give a second glance.

Notes on Contributors

Jenny Barden trained as an artist, then a lawyer, and for several years worked for one of the leading firms of commercial solicitors in the City of London. Chance research into a painting triggered a passion for writing. Journeys in South and Central America then led to ideas for a novel set in the New World during the Age of Discovery. That novel is now close to completion, and *Propitiation* derives from one of the chapters in an early draft. Jenny is represented by Jonathan Pegg of the Jonathan Pegg Literary Agency. For more about her writing visit: www.jennybarden.com

Claudia Boers is originally from Johannesburg and now lives in London. She left behind a career in fashion to focus on writing in 2007. She's been published in Your Messages (a collection of flash fiction) and was commended in the Ilkley Short Story Competition 2008. Claudia's currently working on her first collection of short stories and is fascinated by the imperfect roundness of life.

Ben Cheetham lives and writes in Sheffield. His short fiction has been published or is forthcoming in The London Magazine, Dream Catcher, Staple, Transmission, Momaya Annual Review 2008, Swill, Hoi Polloi and various other magazines.

Carys Davies's short stories have won prizes in national and international competitions, including the Bridport, Asham, Orange/Harpers & Queen and Fish. They have been published in magazines and anthologies and broadcast on BBC Radio 4. Her debut collection of short stories *Some New Ambush* (Salt, 2007) was one of ten books longlisted for the 2008 Wales Book of the Year Prize and was also a Finalist in the 2008 Calvino Prize in the US. She lives in Lancaster with her husband and four children.

Carol Farrelly is currently a student of Glasgow University's MLitt in Creative Writing. She has lived in Italy, London, Oxford and Brighton. Italy and London are the places she still misses. She has had several short stories published in magazines such as *Litro* and *Random Acts of Writing*.

Nick Holdstock's work has appeared in *Edinburgh Review*, *Stand,* and *The Southern Review.* He recently edited the *Stolen Stories* anthology. www.nickholdstock.com

Jo Lloyd grew up in Wales and now lives in Oxford. Her stories have been longlisted for the Bridport and Asham prizes. She is not [sic] working on a novel. Update: "Work" by Jo Lloyd was awarded first prize in the Willesden Herald short story competition 2009.

Margot Taylor is an ex lollipop lady who lives with her husband and two teenagers in Somerset, UK. Her spare time is divided between her passions for boating, running on the nearby Quantock Hills, and writing short stories. "Ebb Tide" is her first published story.

Jill Widner was the recipient of a 2007 Artist Trust/ Washington State Arts Commission fellowship; she was a resident at Yaddo in 2007 and 2008; and she is a graduate of the Iowa Writers' Workshop. "Mina and

Fina and Lotte Wattimena" is an excerpt from her novel in progress, *The Smell of Sulphur*, which fictionalizes her experience growing up in Indonesia in the 1960s. Other excerpts have been published or are forthcoming in North American Review, Hobart (online), and Kyoto Journal. Her fiction has also appeared recently in Memoir (and), 971 Menu, and Hitotoki (New York). She lives in Yakima, Washington.

Morowa Yejidé is a native of Washington, D.C. She was educated at Kalamazoo College, where she received her degree in International Relations, and graduated from an international exchange program at Waseda University in Tokyo, Japan. Her short stories have appeared in the Istanbul Literary Review, Ascent Aspirations Magazine, The Taj Mahal Review, and Underground Voices, and others. Her stories often focus on the layers of relationships and the inner landscapes of her characters' minds. Tokyo Chocolate is a tapestry of her own experiences and impressions. She currently lives in Atlanta, Georgia with her husband and three sons.